# AT DEATH'S DOOR

# AT DEATH'S DOOR

A JUNIPER GROVE MYSTERY

KARIN KAUFMAN

# CHAPTER 1

"Smell that heavenly turkey," Julia said, a look of pleasure and anticipation on her face. "Stuffing, fresh-baked bread."

I nodded, agreeing with her assessment. "And mashed potatoes with sour cream and chives."

"You can smell that?"

"No, I'm just hoping."

A young woman who introduced herself as the caterer and then promptly disappeared had invited us inside Nora Barberton's home, and now we stood just inside her double front doors, relishing the warmth of the house and the aromas of Thanksgiving dinner. Our momentary reverie was interrupted by a man approaching us with outstretched arms. "May I take your coats?"

"Yes, please," I said. Julia and I shed our coats and handed them to him, and he draped them neatly over his right arm.

"Julia, you're here!" a woman cried out. "How lovely!" She strode across the spacious living room, the ends of her long green scarf spreading like wings across her arms.

It was Nora Barberton, I figured. I hadn't met her yet, but she fit Julia's description. Short but stylish gray hair, glasses. She was seventy-five, Julia had told me, but the woman I saw heading our way moved briskly, with the strong, smooth gait of youth.

"I wouldn't miss Thanksgiving at the Barberton house for anything in the world," Julia said, giving Nora a hug.

"And you must be Rachel," Nora said, turning to me. "I'm Nora. I'm so glad you could come. I see you've given your coats to Dominic Larson, our unofficial butler this afternoon."

Still holding our coats, Dominic gave a small bow, though with his considerable height—he was at least six foot three—it became a stately gesture. "Glad to help, ladies. I'll be seeing you later." He pivoted, imitating the fussy precision of a manservant, and disappeared down a hallway with our coats.

"He's my financial adviser in real life," Nora said. "He's here with his wife, Sheila, but you'll meet her later. Now, you two come with me. We were all about to visit the documents room. My cataloger has discovered something simply astonishing. And yes, Julia, we'll be eating soon." She swallowed a smile and peered over the tops of her glasses at Julia.

"I'm not the one whose stomach growled all the way here," Julia said, tilting her head at me.

I put my hand to my stomach. "That's only because it's empty. I wanted to make sure I saved room."

"Don't let Julia tease you," Nora said. "This isn't my first Thanksgiving with her. She can put away food like a teenage boy." She spun on her heels and marched to the middle of the living room, where she paused and politely cleared her throat. "Attention, everyone. My dear friend Julia Foster and her friend Rachel Stowe have arrived. All eight of us are here, so as promised, we're off to the documents room. Please leave your drinks behind. Kendra, would you do the honors?"

A young, dark-haired woman set her glass of wine on a side table and beckoned for the assembled guests to follow her up a staircase to the second floor. Nora cut across the living room to where an elderly woman stood, and she gestured at an armchair, imploring the woman to sit. The woman would have none of it. She shook her head, pointed at the stairs, and painstakingly made her way to the first step. Glancing about her, Nora caught sight of Dominic and spread her arms in exasperation. He laughed and mouthed, "I've got it."

Julia leaned my way. "That's the woman I told you about," she said. "Anne Rightler. She lives at Aspen Glen, an assisted living home, but Julia invites her for dinner once a month and on holidays. I don't think she wants her climbing the stairs."

I could see why. At the bottom of the staircase, Anne was having trouble negotiating her way onto that crucial first step. She took hold of the banister. She let go and wrapped her bulky brown cardigan about her as if needing its comfort. She raised and then lowered her leg. Dominic swept around her and offered her his arm, which he handily slid under her armpit, giving her the lift she needed. Once in motion, Anne made the successive steps with less difficulty. Julia, Nora, and I followed them to a hallway at the top of the stairs, where the other dinner guests waited for us.

"Are we all here?" Kendra said.

"What about your caterer?" Dominic asked. "Paige, I think?"

"She's in the kitchen," Nora replied. "Said she couldn't leave the turkey."

"All right, then," Kendra said, taking us down the hall. She stopped at an open door and flicked a wall switch, and light flooded the room before us.

"Oh, my goodness," Anne said. "So much brighter than when I was here last."

It was a large room of shining white cabinets with beveled glass doors and brilliant white bookshelves, eclipsing the soft glow of the November sun as it slanted through two casement windows.

Kendra stood next to the room's single desk and eagerly waved everyone inside. "It is brighter, Anne. And not only that, but these lights are much safer to use around old papers and books. They don't cause fading the way the old lights did. During spring and summer we close the drapes, of course."

Anne nodded. "Keeping them safe is the most important thing."

Kendra squeezed her hands together and let her gaze travel slowly around the room, milking the moment a little too much, I thought. "Most of you know that Nora possesses some of the finest documents, books, and memorabilia on early Colorado history in the state, including on Ceran St. Vrain, who founded the famous fort that bears his name. Until last week, I'd only discovered secondary documents concerning St. Vrain—letters from one of his daughters, and so on. Then I discovered something remarkable." She glanced at Nora and all eyes turned her way.

"It was hidden away in an old box," Nora said. "I had no idea. My husband never told me. I suppose he thought I wouldn't be interested."

Kendra took a few steps toward the cabinets, opened one of the doors, and reached inside, her unhurried movements calculated to let Nora's guests know that what they were about to behold was beyond special. When she swung back, she held a tiny oval painting between her palms.

Dominic gasped. "Are you saying . . . ?"

Kendra grinned. "It's a miniature, watercolor on ivory, under glass in its original frame, painted by Henry Dobbs in 1840. I'm able to say with certainty now that this is a previously unknown contemporary portrait of Ceran St. Vrain. He and Dobbs met in Washington, D.C. in that very year."

A red-haired woman wrapped an arm around Dominic's waist and leaned close to the miniature, using his tall frame for support. "That must be very valuable—and not just historically."

"The redhead is Sheila Larson, Dominic's wife," Julia whispered.

"It had better be," I whispered back.

"It's very precious?" Anne asked.

"Yes, it is," Kendra said.

Nora, who had been standing at the back of our little crowd, now marched up to Kendra and took the portrait from her, grasping it between her forefinger and thumb. Kendra winced.

"I think it's time to update your insurance," Dominic said.

His wife, who nodded vigorously, seemed to concur.

"I already have," Nora said, gazing at the ivory.

Dominic's eyes shot from the portrait to Nora.

"Though it's the historical value that interests me," Nora went on. "But with Kendra's documentation, the insurance company suggested sixty thousand dollars."

"Which insurance company?" Dominic asked.

Nora looked up. "Oh, Dominic, I went with a specialist. I meant to tell you."

"A specialist? It doesn't need surgery, it needs insurance."

"I suggested Williams and Associates," Kendra said. "They're experts on the monetary value of historical artwork."

Ignoring Kendra, Dominic kept his eyes riveted to Nora. "I could have found that out for you. All you had to do was ask."

Kendra persisted. "It's one item, Dominic. You're insuring everything else."

Dominic's eyes narrowed as he turned them on Kendra. "And everything else in this room is worth two-thirds of what that single item is. You know I make part of my living on referrals. You did this deliberately."

"Dominic, not now," Sheila Larson pleaded, taking hold of his arm.

"Let's stop," Nora said. She set the miniature on the desk, positioning it like a paperweight atop a short stack of papers, and again Kendra winced. "Let's go eat before we ruin Thanksgiving."

"It's a little late for that," Dominic said. "For me, at least, though I'm sure Kendra's having a great day."

"That's enough," a man behind me said. He pushed past me and reached Kendra in two long strides. "My wife has done a terrific job, and I think she should be congratulated."

"What are you talking about?" Dominic said. "The portrait was always here. All she did was open the right box. If anyone else had access to this room—"

"But no one else does because it's my wife who was

chosen to catalog the collection. She's what people call a professional."

Dominic took a menacing step forward. "A professional what, Ben? That's the question."

"Spell it out, Dominic," the man said, tugging at the knot of his own red tie. "Don't be coy. Say it."

Although Ben was a good three inches shorter than Dominic, he was a decade younger, and his posturing suggested he considered himself more than a match for the older man. Afraid the two were about to come to blows, Julia and I backstepped our way toward the door. "I gave up a night in front of the TV for this?" I said under my breath.

"Think of it as research," Julia said. "Something you can put in one of your mystery novels."

"I don't want research, I want mashed potatoes."

Both wives now latched on to their husbands, begging them to calm down, and for a brief moment, Nora foolishly stepped between them, risking a misplaced upper cut to her chin. In that instant, I saw Anne grab the miniature from the desk and slip it into her cardigan's pocket.

I sucked in my breath. "Did you see that?"

"See what?" Julia said.

Wearing a self-satisfied smile, and ignored by everyone but me, Anne ambled out of the room.

"Julia, I don't believe it. Anne just stole that miniature."

"She what?"

Julia and I backed out of the room and looked down the hall. Anne was making her way for the staircase.

"The stairs." I dashed down the hall and caught up with Anne at the head of the stairs. "Anne, stop. You'll fall."

She looked up at me, the picture of innocence and

kindness. "Then you'll have to help me, won't you? I was waiting for you. I'd never take the stairs by myself."

We slowly made our way down the stairs, Julia to one side of Anne and me to the other, our arms around her waist—and me dreading to think what would happen if she stumbled and we lost hold of her. I sighed in relief when we made it to the living room.

"Thank you, both of you," Anne said. She started for an armchair but stopped to look back at Julia. "I know you, don't I?"

"We've met many times, dear," Julia said, giving Anne's shoulder a rub. "I'm Julia Foster, Nora's friend."

Anne seemed perplexed. "How long have you been friends with Nora?"

"More than thirty years."

"Doesn't time go by fast? I've been at Aspen Glen for thirty years."

"I think about ten years," Julia said.

"I'm eighty-seven, I know that."

"That's right, dear."

I was beginning to understand. Anne may have taken the miniature, but she wasn't responsible for her actions.

"I'll sit now," she said, placing her hands on the arms of the chair. She lowered herself gently, but in the final few inches before touchdown, she dropped like a stone. I cringed, thinking of the miniature in her sweater pocket. "Come here," she instructed, wiggling her fingers at me.

I sat in the chair nearest hers, wondering how to broach the subject of the very expensive painting she was quite possibly now sitting on.

"I told you I was waiting for you," she said.

"Yes, by the stairs."

"This isn't about stairs. What's your name again?"

"Rachel Stowe."

Anne nodded. "That's right. Nora told me about you. You're the detective."

"I'm a mystery writer."

"Six of one, five dozen of the other. Nora needs your help." She glanced about the living room and, satisfied that no one could hear her, she said, "There's a thief in this house."

I glanced at Julia.

"No, no," Anne said. She patted her sweater pocket. "I'm not talking about me. I'm not the thief."

# CHAPTER 2

I was speechless. A couple minutes earlier Anne hadn't been able to recall Julia's face, but now, in talking of this thief in the house, she spoke with perfect clarity. Still, it was Anne who had so brazenly pocketed the miniature. Was this elderly woman just terribly confused? "Are you sure about this thief?" I asked.

"You have to tell Nora," she answered, dismissing my question. "She needs to hear from a detective."

Now we were back to me being a detective. I didn't know what to think.

"And I know exactly who the thief is," Anne said.

The sound of shattering glass broke the silence in the living room.

"Who's there?" Anne called out. "Who's listening?"

I heard a scraping sound, like glass on tile, and a moment later a blonde-haired woman dressed in a crisp white shirt and black vest crept around an archway wall, cradling a broken wine glass in her hand. "It's only me. I was having a sip in the kitchen."

"You're the caterer," I said.

"Yeah, Paige Calloway of Calloway Catering. We met at the door." She glanced down at the glass. "That's a few bucks less in my paycheck tonight."

The red blotch on her thumb was far too bright for wine. "You cut yourself," I said, rising from my chair.

Paige stared down at her hand. "I guess I did."

"Nora's got something in her bathroom for that," Julia said. "I'll be right back."

As Julia headed for the staircase, Nora and the other guests began to descend the stairs. Their argument, at least for the time being, was over, as Nora was detailing the dinner menu to a chorus of appreciative oohs and ahhs. I followed Paige into the kitchen to grab a paper towel for her hand and help her sweep up whatever broken glass remained on the floor.

At first glance, Paige had told the truth about taking a wine break. There was an open bottle of red wine on the kitchen island and a couple small shards of glass on the tile floor between the island and the sink. But when I swung back to pull a paper towel from a holder on the counter, I saw a puddle of wine near the archway. So how was it Paige had broken the glass near the island but wine from that glass had ended up fifteen feet away?

I handed Paige the paper towel, tore two more from the holder, and then strode to the puddle and mopped it up. When I turned back, she looked quickly away and insisted she needed to get on with her work or the turkey would be ruined. "It needs to come out of the oven and rest," she said.

"Need help?"

"I work alone."

The puddle of wine spoke for itself, so I decided not to mention it. Obviously, Paige had been listening in, but that wasn't uncommon for a caterer at a dinner party. "Can I ask you something?" I said. "Do you know Anne Rightler?"

"Not really. I've served her dinner." Paige busied

herself with basting the turkey, refusing to pause or look me in the eye. She was young—in her early thirties, I thought—with fair, smooth skin, a straight nose, and the kind of well-defined jawline that seemed to disintegrate after age forty.

"You've served her here?"

"Yeah. Nora invites her for dinner once a month."

"She hires you for the dinner?"

"A year now."

"Did you hear the guests upstairs arguing?"

Paige squeezed the last of the juices from the baster, set it on the island, and then turned my way with a roll of her eyes. "Every single time they get together there's an argument over something."

"Really? Like what?"

"Usually about that room upstairs, or sometimes about donating Nora's things to a local museum—that kind of thing. The Wallaces and Larsons are always at each other. But what it comes down to every time is money, which is hilarious since they all have more of it than most people."

"I don't understand. Why would they argue over money? Are they investing in stocks together or something like that?"

"Not that I know of, though Nora lets Dominic Larson control her money way too much." Paige seemed relieved that I wasn't going to mention the wine by the archway, and she seized on the new subject with relish. "Dominic's the tall guy with black hair. He's Nora's financial adviser."

"He and Ben Wallace got into a pretty heated argument."

"Not for the first time. See, Dominic controls the actual money, but Kendra controls the asset money—you know, the historical stuff in the documents room. Both of them want it *all.*"

"I still don't understand why they're at odds."

Paige searched Nora's refrigerator and came away with a plastic-wrapped block of white cheese, which she plopped down on the kitchen island. "Kendra and Ben consider themselves the experts. She's the cataloger with a degree and he's a lecturer in history, writing a book on this St. Vrain guy. Experts, see? They want Nora's money so they can preserve her collection and even buy more historical stuff. But Dominic thinks they're wasting her money—and it's money he wants to invest and make a commission on."

"You've picked all this up just by listening to them?"

"Like I said, they argue all the time, and always about the same stuff."

"I've got a Band-Aid and antiseptic ointment," Julia announced as she entered the kitchen. "You shouldn't handle food with a cut, Paige."

Paige stuck her injured hand in the air. "I'm not using the bloody hand."

"Except when she took the turkey out of the oven, and then she used potholders," I said with a smile.

Julia made a face. "Still . . ."

"Thanks, though," Paige said, taking the Band-Aid and ointment from Julia.

"Any fights break out in the living room?" I asked.

"Not yet," Julia said. "When I walked through the living room I heard Anne telling everyone about this thief among us."

Paige wavered for an instant, but she recovered quickly and proceeded to peel back the wrapper on her Band-Aid. "Sorry, guys, I'm going to have to ask you to leave. I've got five minutes before dinner is served and loads to do still."

"Of course," I said, pulling Julia away from the turkey platter. "Don't you have an assistant?"

"Can't afford one."

"Are there mashed potatoes, by any chance?"

"Already cooked, chopped, and ready for the food processor."

Julia and I headed into the living room, but I pulled her aside before we joined the others. "I'm positive Paige dropped the wineglass when she heard Anne talk about a thief," I whispered. "She was listening."

"What are we going to do about the miniature Anne took?"

"We have to tell Nora. We can't let Anne leave with it, and we can't let her keep it in her pocket. She's *sitting* on sixty thousand dollars."

"Julia, Rachel," Dominic said, shouting and waving at us as though we were a football field away. "Come on over here. Where are your wine glasses?"

I reluctantly left the safety of the staircase for a couch seat in the living room alongside Dominic and his wife, Sheila. I saved the armchair next to the couch for Julia. She looked worried about Nora and Anne—and not in the mood to sit next to the fidgety Sheila, who was furiously twisting a lock of her red hair between her fingers.

"Would either of you like wine?" Dominic asked, glancing from Julia to me.

Julia declined, but I asked for a small glass of white. As Dominic headed to the kitchen, it struck me that Nora or one of her guests had to have seen that the miniature was missing from the documents room before they headed back downstairs. After all, they had remained upstairs, arguing, for several minutes after Julia and I left. Why had no one said anything? Nora would never have left that room without a last look at the precious painting. And for that matter, where was Anne? She'd left the living room and was who-knows-where in the house—possibly dropping or scratching the miniature.

I excused myself and headed to a separate little seating area where Nora was talking with Kendra and Ben Wallace. Nora looked up, smiled, and patted the couch seat next to hers.

"Nora, can I talk to you a minute?" I said, sinking into the overly soft cushion.

"By all means," she said.

Intrigued, Kendra and Ben leaned in, moving in unison. They were both in their late thirties, but that's where the similarity ended. Kendra had dark, wavy hair, while Ben's was light brown with fledgling touches of gray, and Ben's strong, straight nose and wide jaw was a counterpoint to Kendra's more delicate features. "I meant privately," I said apologetically.

"No problem," Ben said, rising from his chair. "Nora, would you like more wine?"

"No, thank you."

"We'll talk later," Kendra said. "I've got some other ideas I want to run past you."

"Why don't you go into the dining room?" Nora said. "We're about ready to start."

"Here comes Dominic," Ben said.

"Ignore him," Kendra said, laying a hand on Ben's arm.

Dominic was heading for our little group, a glass of white wine in his hand.

"He's bringing me the wine I asked for," I said,

thinking that explaining his approach would assure Ben that Dominic's aim was not to continue their argument. But Dominic's eyes were shooting daggers: he was ready for another go. I sprang from my couch—not an easy thing, given its oatmeal-like softness—and cut him off before he could reach Ben.

"Thank you," I said, taking hold of the glass. An instant later I spun him around with a push to his shoulder. "Would you please get Julia a small glass of white?"

He gave me a puzzled look over his shoulder. "But she said she didn't want any."

"She says that to be polite." I gave his shoulder a gentle shove, and off he went, though not without giving me another expression of bewilderment.

I retook my seat on the couch and mumbled another apology at Kendra and Ben, which the couple finally took as their cue to leave.

"I'm sorry about that," I said to Nora when they'd gone, "but this is serious. Did you notice that your miniature had been taken from the documents room?"

Nora smiled wearily, the skin around her eyes crinkling into even deeper crow's feet. "Yes, Rachel, I did. I thought for sure she'd take something else. She knows how rare that piece is."

"Did anyone else notice it was missing?"

"Everyone did."

"Does Anne still have it, then? Where is she?"

"I haven't taken it back yet. I need to find a quiet moment so I don't embarrass her. She went off to the restroom. I'm only hoping she doesn't drop it on the tiles." Pursing her lips, she shook her head. "I should have kept my eye on it."

"I'm getting the feeling that Anne has done this before."

Nora looked me square in the eye. "The past four times she's been here, in September, October, and twice this month. We've all gotten quite used to it."

"She steals from you?"

"She returns everything before she leaves. She says she's protecting my things, but when I ask her from what or from whom, she says she doesn't know." Nora let her eyes stray over the living room before looking back to me. "Except tonight. Tonight's different. She was excited when I told her Julia Foster's friend, the one who solves murders, would be here. She says she knows now who the thief is."

"Nora, is it possible the thief is Anne? She seems like a sweet woman, but she's, she's . . ." I searched for a kind way to put it.

"She's not all there?"

"To be honest, no."

A shout came from somewhere on the first floor, jolting me. There was another shout, and then another. At first insistent, the shouts became a frantic alarm.

"That's Kendra," Nora said, struggling to get up from the couch.

I jumped to my feet and helped Nora get to hers. Julia, too, was rising from her armchair, and Dominic and Sheila were staring at each other on the couch. An instant later, Ben and Paige came flying out of the kitchen, Ben swiveling this way and that in the living room, uncertain which way to go.

"The hall," Nora said, gesticulating wildly.

Ben raced for the hall, Paige and Dominic on his heels, and was rapidly followed by Nora, Julia, and me. I had to push my way around Sheila, who halted halfway down the hall, refusing to take another step.

At the end of the long hallway, Kendra was riveted to the floor, staring through an open doorway into what I thought must be a bedroom.

"The cellar stairs," Nora said, her voice filled with dread.

I stopped short, not wanting to see what I knew Kendra saw.

Kendra looked at Ben, her eyes wild. She pointed. "Anne's down there. I think she's dead."

# CHAPTER 3

"She fell all the way down. It looked like her neck was broken," Nora said, dabbing at her tears with a cloth napkin Paige had retrieved from the dining room. "Was it?"

"I don't know, ma'am," Chief James Gilroy said.

"What was she doing going down the stairs?"

"I don't know that either."

"Did she fall, or . . . ?"

"We'll find out." Gilroy stood, leaving Nora and Paige on the couch, and walked over to Underhill, who was trying without success to comfort Sheila Larson on the other side of the living room. Either Dominic hadn't tried to soothe her frazzled nerves or he'd given up, and Kendra and Ben Wallace, stone-faced and silent, were ignoring her completely.

I could have told Nora she'd get nothing but terse replies from Gilroy. It wasn't his style to speculate. When we'd first met—after I'd discovered a body in my backyard—I had judged him cold and unfeeling, but I couldn't have been more wrong. He was a quiet and thoughtful man, that's all, and he was too good a cop to divulge even a single fact of the case to a room full of possible suspects.

Gilroy had taken all our statements, such as they were.

We had all lost sight of Anne not long after Julia came downstairs with the bandage and ointment for Paige, and very shortly after she told everyone there was a thief in the house. No one had paid much attention to where she'd gone or how long she'd been gone. Nora told Gilroy that Anne had asked where the restroom was—having forgotten its location again—and she'd directed her down the hall. Anne had gone a door too far.

"I keep that cellar door shut for just this reason," Nora said. "You open it and you're at death's door. Those steps are horribly steep."

Julia took Gilroy's seat on the couch and wrapped an arm around Nora's shoulder. "It's not your fault. Anne opened the wrong door. She wasn't paying attention. You know how she is. How many times has she used the restroom on this floor?"

"A lot," Nora murmured.

"And still she forgot where it was."

*But did she forget?* I wondered. Even if she had forgotten and by chance opened the wrong door, what had sent her plunging down a flight of stairs? Anne was forgetful, not blind. She wouldn't have opened the cellar door, seen the steps, and then thought the restroom was now at the bottom of those steps. No. Realizing her mistake, she would have shut the cellar door and opened another door and another until she found the restroom.

"She wouldn't have tried to go down those steps," I said with certainty.

Paige seemed startled by my remark, and Julia glared at me as though I'd woken a baby she'd just rocked to sleep.

"Julia, remember how she waited for us at the top of the stairs," I said, "after she left the documents room? She knew she couldn't go up or down the stairs without help. Her memory was bad, but was she foolish? Nora?"

Nora twisted one end of her scarf, wringing it in her hands like a wet dish towel. "No, not at all. People assumed she was foolish because she was eighty-seven, but apart from her memory lapses, she was sharp."

"How can you be sharp without memory?" Paige said with a scowl.

"When we played cards," Nora said, "Anne kept track of every card dealt. With four people playing. Could you do that? I never could. Just because Anne couldn't remember where the bathroom was because she hadn't seen it for a week doesn't mean she couldn't see and understand what was right in front of her."

"And the steps were right in front of her," Julia said softly.

"Even if Anne couldn't remember the right door, she had enough sense not to think the restroom was in the cellar," I added a little too loudly. "She didn't fall." Julia put a finger to her lips to caution me, and I turned to look over my shoulder. Our voices had carried across the living room, to where the Larsons and the Wallaces were listening with rapt attention. Gilroy, too, had stopped jotting in his notebook and was watching me.

Ben shifted in his seat and threw his left arm over the back of the couch for a better look at the opinionated woman across the room. "And you've known Anne for how long?" he asked.

"Long enough," I said.

"She's right, Ben," Nora said, speaking as loudly as I had moments ago. "Anne wouldn't have tried to walk down those stairs. That doesn't make sense."

"Anne did a lot of things that didn't make sense," Kendra said, supporting her husband. "Anyway, what else could have happened?" She looked around the room, waiting for a response. Dominic shrugged, and Ben, figuring he and his wife had scored a point, turned back around in his seat.

And they'd claimed to be Anne's friends. She deserved better. "Someone could have pushed her," I said.

Kendra glared at me. "Don't be ridiculous," she snapped.

"One of us, presumably?" Dominic said.

"I don't want to hear this," Sheila said.

"Or maybe it was you, Rachel," Dominic said.

"Let's be quiet so we can go home," Sheila said.

"I mean, you're the visitor here, not us," Dominic added. "If we wanted to push Anne down the stairs, we could have done it weeks or months ago."

I couldn't decide if he was trying to taunt me for my outburst or his wife for her timidity. He seemed to be getting pleasure out of doing both. And Gilroy, silent as usual, was watching and listening. He knew how many criminals slipped up and implicated themselves by talking too much.

"I think the coroner can say whether she was pushed," Kendra said. "What's taking the man so long, anyway?" she asked, her eyes darting down the hall. "It's creepy, thinking of him down there, examining Anne's body."

"Oh, Kendra," Nora chided.

I didn't care how long the coroner took to do his job. I was just grateful he was at the end of the hall and down a long flight of stairs and I didn't have to hear or see what he was doing.

"It's obvious no one here killed her," Dominic said. "We've all been here or in the kitchen since we came downstairs."

"That's right," Kendra said. "Only Anne went down the hall. None of us have moved."

"That's not true, Kendra," I said. "For instance, when I got up to talk to Nora, Dominic and Sheila were sitting where you and Ben are sitting now."

"I went to the kitchen for your friend's wine," Dominic said. "You sent me. Remember?"

"So why not return to your seat next to Sheila? Why did she move? Why did Kendra and Ben take your seats?"

"Hang on just a minute, lady," Ben said.

Kendra was about to chime in when I held up my hands. "I'm only saying there's been a lot more moving around than Dominic claims."

Sheila sniffed loudly, and Dominic, in the first husbandly move he'd made all evening, handed her his handkerchief.

"We never even had Thanksgiving dinner," she said before blowing her nose.

"I was in the middle of carving my turkey," Underhill groused. "It's all cold now."

Gilroy briefly shut his eyes and pinched the bridge of his nose, probably to stop himself from saying something to Underhill. His officer was overworked, but he was letting the world know it at every opportunity, including the most inappropriate moments.

We were all missing Thanksgiving. I'd been looking forward to it. Gilroy and I had met for coffee three weeks ago, and for lunch two weeks after that, so I'd madly thought I would invite him to Thanksgiving at Nora's house—a stress-free, no-pressure place for us to move to the next step in dating: dinner. So much for plans.

It wasn't his fault our relationship—and I was pretty sure I couldn't call it that yet—was moving at a glacial pace. The Juniper Grove Police Department was still a man short, and because Gilroy insisted there be someone on duty at the station every day until midnight, he and Underhill were still stretched to their limits. Gilroy had thought the post would be filled by Thanksgiving. But apparently, qualified officers preferred the higher pay of Colorado's larger cities. Little Juniper Grove, nestled against the foothills of the Rockies, with a population of twelve hundred and a tiny budget to match, couldn't compete.

"Chief Gilroy, can I make coffee?" Paige asked.

"Sure," he answered.

As Paige made her way to the kitchen, Underhill tracked her with his eyes, and when she drew near, he raised a finger as if summoning a waiter. "Can I?"

"Yup," she said, disappearing through the archway.

"We've all told you everything we know," Ben said, rubbing his sizable jaw. "There's nothing else to add. Can't we go home?"

"Just a couple more things and you can all leave," Gilroy said.

"Thank goodness!" Sheila exclaimed.

"I'd like to see the documents room, Mrs. Barberton," Gilroy said.

Ben groaned.

"Of course," Nora said, getting to her feet.

"If you don't mind, I can go by myself," he said, no doubt in deference to Nora's age. He hadn't seen her earlier, mounting the steps with the energy of a woman twenty years younger.

"Absolutely, please do," Nora said.

"Is it locked?" Gilroy asked.

"No, but that's going to change."

"Have you had a break-in?"

"Nothing like that."

"Anything stolen, then?"

"No, but I have many irreplaceable items in that room."

Kendra and Ben exchanged sidelong glances.

"What sort of irreplaceable items?" Gilroy said.

"The kind of records researchers love," Kendra said, answering for Nora.

Ben nodded vigorously. "And museums covet. One-of-a-kind historical records."

"Oh, brother," Dominic said.

Anger flashed across Ben's face. "What would you know, Dominic? Are you a history professor?"

"You're a lecturer, Ben, not a professor. You don't even work on the main campus. Stop giving yourself a promotion."

Dominic's words must have struck a sore spot with Ben, because he jerked forward and perched himself on the edge of his seat, his arms twitching as though he couldn't decide whether to remain seated or rise and fight.

I glanced at Gilroy. He was giving them all free rein—and taking in their every word, their every movement. Did he too suspect that Anne's death wasn't an accident?

"At least I don't make my living by pushing useless investments," Ben said.

"Stop it, you two," Nora said, tears shining in her eyes. "Not in my house. If you want to fight, do it outside. But if you do, never come back. Do you understand? I've had it with both of you."

Nora's threat, followed almost immediately by the

appearance of two paramedics pushing an empty gurney into the living room, brought an end to Ben and Dominic's argument.

Underhill roused himself, took a quick peek around the archway—probably seeking his coffee—and then escorted the paramedics down the hall. "This is a tough one, guys. You have to go down some pretty steep steps, so watch yourselves."

Rather than head upstairs for a look at the documents room, Gilroy stayed downstairs and continued to keep an eye on everyone. We sat quietly, listening to muffled sounds from the cellar, the only relief coming when Paige announced there was plenty of coffee in the kitchen and she'd packaged leftover turkey and vegetables for anyone who wanted to take some home.

At last I could hear the gurney wheeling down the hall. Kendra must have caught sight of it, because she turned her face away and feigned interest in a rather ordinary table lamp.

In an effort to distract Nora, Paige quickly handed her a cup of coffee, but Nora refused.

"Chief Gilroy," Nora said, pushing to her feet, "I've just remembered that Anne has a very precious miniature painting in the pocket of her cardigan."

"She what?" Kendra said, looking back from the lamp.

The coroner entered the living room two steps ahead of the gurney and started for the front door.

"She took it from the documents room," Nora said.

Gilroy halted the paramedics. "Are you saying she stole it?"

"I saw her take it and put it in her sweater pocket," I said.

"There was nothing in her pockets," the coroner said.

Nora spun back to him, incredulous. "She put the miniature in her pocket. I know she did."

"I was with Dr. Reardon when he searched her pockets," Gilroy said. "There was nothing there."

"We're talking about a painting?" Reardon asked.

"A very small and expensive one," Kendra replied.

"It was there," Nora insisted.

"She may have put it there," Reardon said, "but it's not there now, and it wasn't anywhere near her body." He turned to Gilroy. "I haven't left her side since I got here."

Gilroy nodded. "Mrs. Barberton, is it possible Mrs. Rightler put the painting somewhere else?"

"No, she wouldn't have. She thought she was protecting it."

"From what?" Dominic said.

"From one of you!" Nora shouted.

Everyone halted. Even Underhill, at last savoring his cup of coffee, stood frozen with the cup halfway to his mouth.

"Do you want the truth?" Nora said. "*That's* the truth! I didn't want to believe it, but one of you has been stealing from me, and you killed Anne because she knew."

# CHAPTER 4

I made coffee while Julia began to clear my kitchen table. We'd taken leftovers from Nora's house back to mine, at last having, though not enjoying, our Thanksgiving dinner. We had both resisted the urge to knock on Holly Kavanagh's door—she lived across the street from us on Finch Hill Road—and tell her what had happened. It was Thanksgiving evening, after all. Holly worked six days a week at her bakery, Holly's Sweets, and she deserved a quiet holiday with her family.

"It's not right that Anne died that way," Julia said, setting the plates and silverware in the sink. "She was a kind woman. She didn't deserve it."

I pulled two mugs from the cabinet above the coffeemaker. "So you don't think she fell?"

"I was just saying that for Nora's benefit. Anne always waited for help at the stairs. I was at Nora's just last month when Anne was there. It was the same as tonight—she waited for help. She wasn't a fool."

The aroma of fresh-brewed coffee filled the kitchen, mingling with the dinner smells of sage dressing and turkey. I was tired but restless. I needed to go over the day and its events with Julia, and I sensed that she, too, wanted to talk. "Let's take our coffee into the living room. I'm in the mood for a nice warm fire."

After a couple false starts, I got a good blaze going in the fireplace, and I settled into one of my two couches, Julia taking the one closest to the fire. The dry wood snapped and sparked, and the fire cast a warm glow over the room. For a while, neither of us talked. We sipped at our coffees, letting the fire soothe our still-jangled nerves.

Julia was the first to break the silence. "How will the coroner determine if Anne was pushed?"

"I don't know."

"I'm afraid he'll say she fell."

"He might. I imagine it's hard to tell the difference."

"She didn't fall, Rachel. You know that."

"I think I do. But I'm not positive."

"What will you do if he says it was an accident?" Julia looked from the fire to me. The firelight illuminated one side of her face and shone through half her short gray hair, highlighting the frizzed ends.

It was a good question. My every instinct was telling me that Anne had been killed by one of Nora's guests. So what would I do if the coroner declared her death an accident? I thought about James Gilroy. About his icy blue eyes glaring in disapproval if I meddled again in matters that didn't concern me. "I'll start by finding out who stood to gain if Anne was murdered—or who stood to lose if she lived."

"The thief would lose," Julia said. "Anne knew who was stealing from Nora, and she announced as much to the whole dinner party."

"I'm not convinced that someone was stealing. Nora took Anne's word for it that things were being stolen from the documents room, but she didn't seem to know *what* had been stolen. Did she ever mention these thefts to you?"

"No, but Nora wouldn't. She's always upbeat at her dinner parties. She would never gather her guests to the table and say, 'Someone is stealing from me. Bon appétit.'"

"Wouldn't Kendra have noticed if someone was taking things? And Dominic was insuring everything except the miniature, so wouldn't he have put in a claim for anything missing?"

Julia turned back to the fire. "Maybe, but there's an awful lot in that room."

"Then again, not everything in the room has been cataloged, or Kendra wouldn't still be working there. Which means not everything has been insured."

"The miniature was insured, thank goodness."

"Now *that's* a mystery," I said, setting my coffee mug on an end table. "What happened to it? I saw Anne put it in her pocket."

"Did you see Ben Wallace's face when Chief Gilroy asked to search his coat?"

I chuckled a little at the memory. "The indignity of it all."

"It's a shame the chief couldn't have Thanksgiving with you at Nora's."

"He and Underhill are working triple time until they find a new officer."

"Oh, but your first Thanksgiving with your boyfriend."

I winced at the word. "Don't say that, Julia. I'm forty-three years old. Women my age don't have boyfriends. Anyway, one coffee and one lunch don't a relationship make."

"He doesn't have coffee with anyone else."

"I'm sure he does."

"You know what I mean."

Headlights swept over my living-room window as a car pulled up the driveway. I reluctantly left the warmth of the fire to answer the front door and found Nora Barberton on my porch, a bottle of wine in one hand and a clutch purse in the other. "This is the only thing I could think of to apologize for interrupting what's left of your Thanksgiving," she said, handing me the bottle. "Can I come in?"

"Nora!" Julia said. "What are you doing here?"

I stepped aside and waved her in. "We were just talking about Anne."

"Good." Without another word, Nora marched to Julia's couch, her scarf waving behind her. I left the bottle on a console table near the door and joined them.

"I have a favor to ask you," Nora said the moment I sat. "I'll pay you whatever you charge. I need you to find that miniature and find out who killed Anne."

"Nora, we only just left your house," I said. "We don't even know Anne's cause of death."

"Then find out who stole the miniature, because whoever took it also killed Anne."

What Nora said made sense. If someone other than the killer had taken it, Anne would have raised a ruckus heard around the house and nothing short of murder would have silenced her. The killer could have reached into Anne's cardigan, grabbed the miniature—with little resistance from Anne—and then shoved her down the stairs in two seconds flat.

"Did Gilroy and Underhill search your house?" I asked.

"Yes, and so did I. The miniature's gone." She dropped her purse on the couch between her and Julia and clenched her fists. "I'm so angry. Not about that painting, but about the betrayal. How many times have those people eaten meals in my house? And to think one of them killed Anne, that poor, lonely woman. Over what? A painting. Money."

"A lot of money," Julia reminded her.

I downed the rest of my coffee, which had gone lukewarm, and tucked my legs beneath me. Suddenly I remembered that I hadn't offered Nora any, but I was feeling bone tired, and I resolved to remain on the couch unless she asked for some. "How would someone go about selling a miniature like that without being caught? I'm sure the insurance company will be on the lookout for anything like it taken to an auction house or even sold on the private market."

"That's if they know about a private sale," Nora said. "There are plenty of collectors flying under the radar. I may never see that miniature again, and Colorado will have lost an important piece of its history."

"I need to know more about how the painting would make it into private hands," I said, "and about how one of your friends would get it there."

Nora's face lit up. "Then you'll try to find it? I knew you would. What about Anne's murderer?"

"Nora, Rachel is right," Julia said. "It's too early. She has to find out what happened to Anne first. Then maybe she can help."

Julia's words seemed to satisfy Nora, and at last she leaned back on the couch, letting her tense muscles relax. "I'll tell you how my so-called friends would sell on the private market. They all have a connection to the historical art and documents world. Kendra is a cataloger and runs the Juniper Grove branch of the Front Range Historical Society,

Ben lectures in history at Northern Colorado Community College and he's writing his PhD dissertation on St. Vrain, Dominic insures art and historical records, and Sheila works at home for a rare books and manuscripts dealer in Fort Collins. They all know people who would pay a lot of money for that miniature without it ever going on the public market."

"I didn't know Sheila was in that world," Julia said.

"Oh yes, and my money's on her as the thief. She has direct access to buyers."

"What about Paige Calloway?" I asked.

"Not Paige," Nora said. "She's a very good caterer, but she knows nothing about history or art."

"That you know of," I said. "Paige told me she's catered special dinners at your house for a year. Is that true?"

"About a year, yes," Nora replied. "I hire her when Anne comes—or when she came. Or when I invite Kendra and the others."

"So Paige has been in your house at least a dozen times in the past year."

"At least." Nora's expression changed in an instant. Now Paige was her number one suspect.

"That's not to say Paige did it," I said, "but we can't rule her out."

"Do you know I never watch any of them?" Nora said. "They have free run—" Nora broke off midsentence as her purse buzzed. She unzipped it, pulled out a phone, and stared at its screen.

"You text?" Julia said.

"Of course I do. I'm not a dinosaur. My neighbor tells me that the police chief is searching my bushes with a flashlight."

"I wonder why," Julia said.

Nora slipped the phone back into her purse. "That's a good question. I thought everyone had left. And don't look so surprised, Julia. I wouldn't drive alone at night without a phone."

"I can't be bothered," Julia said.

"So who's the dinosaur?"

"That was your word, not mine."

"You were never one to keep up with the times."

"You were always one to fall for the trends," Julia said, biting back a grin.

"Only if by trend you mean a wise and convenient advancement."

"Alert the dictionary people. The meaning of trend has now been changed."

Although they were ten or more years apart in age—I'd never gotten an exact handle on Julia's age, since "my early sixties" was as precise as she got—they were like sisters, engaging in the kind of gentle ribbing borne of a long friendship. As I watched them, I felt a little envious. I'd been in Juniper Grove only six months, and though Julia and I had quickly become friends, we didn't have history together. I didn't have history with anyone, really. I'd spent the previous seven years in Boston working as an editor for a publishing company, and that job's long hours and rivalries hadn't made for close friendships. Before leaving Colorado for Boston, I'd spent five years in useless mourning after the man I loved asked me to marry him and then left me a week before the wedding.

"It's funny the police would search my lawn," Nora said.

Suddenly we were back to that. I was on the edge of

falling asleep, so in an effort to rouse myself, I untucked my legs and set my feet flat on the floor.

"Rachel, why would they do that?" Julia asked.

"I think they're looking for the miniature," I said. "The thief couldn't risk taking it with him—or her. If it's not in the house, then someone tossed it out a window to avoid being caught with it. Maybe he planned to come back later and get it."

"Of course!" Julia said. "I told you she was a detective."

"Thank goodness for the glass cover," Nora said. "Imagine the damage if it didn't have one."

I didn't say anything to Nora, but there were two major flaws in my detective work. First, the thief couldn't be sure he'd be able to retrieve the miniature. Rooting around in the bushes a day or two after a murder was a risky thing to do. But more than that, any sensible thief would have waited for a more opportune time. If everyone knew Anne took Nora's things, and that Nora always got them back before Anne left, why not steal the miniature another day? Killing Anne only made escaping with the miniature impossible. I had a feeling that the tiny painting in Anne's pocket was as inconsequential as its size. There was far more going on here.

# CHAPTER 5

"They'll enjoy these," Holly said, setting the last of a dozen donuts into a Holly's Sweets pastry box. "I bet they don't get donuts for breakfast very often."

"Nora tells me it's a nice assisted living home, but it's still assisted living," I said.

"Let me throw in a few extra, no charge."

"And a cream puff for me in a separate bag."

I'd started to tell Holly about Thanksgiving at Nora Barberton's home, but of course she'd already heard the news. At thirty-seven Holly Kavanagh had managed to turn her bakery into Juniper Grove's unofficial meeting place and gossip exchange. Chief Gilroy or Officer Underhill—they alternated days—stopped in every morning, as did the mayor, members of the Board of Trustees, and most of the shop owners on Main Street. Holly's scones, donuts, croissants, and other pastries, including her to-die-for cream puffs, drew them, but they lingered and talked and shared because of the atmosphere. The bakery was bright and warm on dark November mornings, and when you opened the door, you entered a world smelling of sugar and fresh-baked bread.

"Did you hear Gilroy didn't find that little painting?" Holly asked.

I looked up from the pastry display case. "No, I didn't. I wonder where it is."

"Underhill told me they're going to look again this morning. They didn't have enough light last night."

"I hope for Nora's sake they find it."

Holly rang up my donuts and cream puff, and then slid the pink box to me across the counter. "Maybe we could take a box of donuts to Aspen Glen once a month? What do you think?"

"I think that's a great idea."

"I also heard that Nora asked you to find Anne Rightler's killer."

"Who told you that?"

"The mayor."

My mouth dropped open. "How does he know?"

"He's a friend of a friend of hers—or something like that."

"That means Gilroy's heard."

"Probably." Holly grinned. "It's a shame you couldn't have had Thanksgiving dinner with him. Have you decided if you're going to help Nora?"

"I don't even know Anne's cause of death."

"Underhill said she had bruises on both her arms that were consistent with someone grabbing her from behind—hard. They could tell by the position of the thumb impressions, though they couldn't tell if they were from a man or woman's thumbs."

"Underhill talks too much."

Three women entered the bakery and marched straight for the almond and chocolate croissants at the far end of the pastry case. They were on a mission, and Holly was about to get busy. She leaned across the counter and whispered,

"Anne was murdered" before greeting them with a smile.

I'd figured as much, and so had Julia and Nora. And that was the reason I was heading to Aspen Glen. I'd already decided to look into Anne's death.

A phone call from Nora was going to be my entrée. She'd told me last night that she would call first thing this morning and tell the staff I was coming to pick up a quilt from Anne's room. Nora had lent it to her a year ago, and now, as a memento, she wanted it back. While I was there, I'd talk to the residents, bribing them with donuts if necessary, and find out more about Anne.

"Call me tonight," Holly said as I headed for the door. "We'll get the gang together."

"You got it."

The Aspen Glen assisted living home was a mile west of downtown, on a hill surrounded by a small forest of juniper trees. The driveway curved around the front entrance and led to a parking lot at the side of the building. I parked my Forester, grabbed the pastry box, and made my way to the door. I braced myself for a grim tour through a depressing lobby and down dark corridors, but the second I walked inside, my preconceived notions were shattered.

A wood fire burned merrily in the oversized fireplace at the far end of the lobby, where a dozen residents sat on plump armchairs, reading their morning papers and sipping from Wedgwood Blue Willow cups, and a young woman behind the receptionist's desk—*not* wearing a drab institutional uniform—welcomed me, asking if by any chance I was Nora's friend Rachel. I told her I was, and that I thought I'd share some donuts with the residents before I picked up her quilt.

Her eyes on the pink box, she asked, "Is that from

Holly's Sweets?"

"Have one," I said, opening it.

"Thanks! She makes the best donuts in the world." Her hand hovered over the box before finally seizing a chocolate-glazed donut. "You're not out shopping this morning like the rest of the world?"

"Not on your life. Can I ask you something?"

"Ask away," she said, her round, pink face breaking into a grin as she contemplated her treat.

"I met Anne Rightler last night, and she, well . . ." I hesitated, fumbling for the right words. "She had a funny habit of taking Nora's things when she visited. Nora knew about it, of course, and she always got them back before Anne went home."

The woman nodded. Clearly she knew about Anne's strange behavior. "Anne was a sweetheart, and she tried to protect her friends from whatever bad thing she thought would happen to them. Starting about three months ago, she was sure thieves were everywhere."

"Even here?"

"Here and Nora's house. Except for her doctors and nights out with the group, they were the only places she ever went. Last month she entered a friend's room and took a figurine. She'd seen this friend's family there earlier, taking her other belongings home with them." She paused to take a bite of the donut before going on with her story. "This friend was going into hospice, and all she wanted with her were some clothes and her figurine, so her family picked up the rest. Well, Anne thought they were stealing from her and wanted to save the figurine, because she knew how important it was to her friend."

"That's so sad."

"I'm not saying Anne had dementia. Some of our residents do, you know. Anne was forgetful sometimes. Little things, usually, like when to take her pills. But she was fully aware. She just misjudged what she saw and was so eager to help that she acted before questioning what was really going on."

The sound of laughter echoed in the lobby, bouncing off the coffered ceilings, and a grandfather clock chimed the half hour. "Can I ask you one more thing?"

"Sure."

I hesitated again before coming out with it. My question was intrusive, but it had to be asked. "How could Anne afford this place?"

"Didn't Nora tell you?"

"Tell me what?"

"I don't think I can—"

"Are you saying Nora was paying?"

The woman looked from side to side and, satisfied no one could hear her, she said, "She paid for everything, even the extras like our dinner theater nights. She's been an angel."

I'd suspected that Anne didn't have any relatives, at least none that cared for her, or they would have been with her on Thanksgiving. "She didn't have any family?"

"A son somewhere, but he never visited or called, and he sure never paid for anything. We have a few more hardship cases like Anne's, and thankfully, a few more angels like Nora."

I thanked her and started for the fireplace, thinking I'd begin by placing the donut box on a coffee table and then striking up a conversation with anyone willing to talk about Anne. I soon had no shortage of talkers.

"I can't believe she died," an elderly man said after I introduced myself. He passed on the donuts, saying it wasn't good for his blood sugar, but he let me refresh his coffee cup. When I sat down next to him, he told me his name was Frank and that he too knew about Anne's penchant for taking belongings from the other residents' rooms. "None of us were bothered by that, Rachel. We've all got flaws, haven't we? Anne wasn't interested in keeping these things for herself, so in my opinion it wasn't stealing. I had a book go missing from my room some weeks back. I went to Anne's room, and there it was. So I thanked her and took it back."

"Have there ever been any real thefts at Aspen Glen?"

"Not that I've heard of," he said. "Donna? Betty?" He looked across the coffee table.

"Not since I've been here," one of the women said. "I'm Donna, by the way. Anne and I were friends. Were you her friend too?"

"I only met her yesterday, at Nora Barberton's house."

"Yes, Nora." Donna wrapped her sweater more tightly about her body and then held the collar together at her throat, as though she were chilly, even so near the fireplace. "Nora was good to Anne."

"I heard she was."

"Murder is not a fair ending for a woman like Anne," Donna said, her gaunt face and deep-set eyes magnifying the grief in her voice.

I tried to keep my surprise from showing. "How do you know it was murder?"

"We heard she was found at the bottom of some stairs," the other woman said. "And I'm Betty."

"That's right, Betty. Stairs leading down to Nora's cellar."

"Anne *never* took stairs by herself," Donna said. "That's why she lived on the first floor here. She wouldn't go near the stairs unless one or even two of us were helping her."

"But when I was at Nora's house, Anne insisted on going upstairs with the rest of us to visit Nora's documents room."

"Everyone else went?"

"Yes. Nora wanted to show us something."

"Did she wait at the bottom of the stairs for help?" Donna asked.

I thought back. "I think so. I know she waited for help on the way down."

"There you go," Frank said. "It's not that she didn't use the stairs, it's that she didn't like to, and she always waited for help."

"She didn't like to take the elevators, did she, Frank?" Betty asked. "She wanted someone to hold her arm if she did. She was afraid of falling and ending up in a wheelchair."

Frank set down his coffee cup with a sigh. "She never ended up in a wheelchair, thank the Lord."

"Was her eyesight good?" I asked. "Could she have opened a cellar door and not seen the stairs until it was too late?" I needed to explore every possibility, including the possibility that Anne *did* fall and the bruises on her arms had nothing to do with her death.

"Not a chance," Donna said. "She had cataract surgery a year ago—she could see better than any of us. She only needed glasses for reading. You'd have to be blind not to see that stairs are stairs. Worse, you'd have to be a fool, and Anne was not a fool."

Finally capitulating to the lure of the donuts, Betty

grabbed a plain glazed one, tore it in half, and dropped the other half back in the box. "That's what youngsters think. You can't walk or hear as good as you used to, and that makes you senile. Or worse, useless. I'm telling you, I don't think the police care much about finding out who killed her. They never do with someone our age." She took a large bite of her half donut.

"That's not true," I protested. "Chief Gilroy cares, and I'm sure he's determined to solve this case."

"The police chief's a youngster," Frank said.

"He's forty-eight," I countered.

"Like I said, a youngster."

I laughed. Gilroy a youngster? I knew Frank was teasing me—I saw the twinkle in his eye—but from his perspective, Gilroy and I *were* young, and I hadn't thought of myself as young since my fortieth birthday.

"Chief Gilroy is half Charlie's age," Betty said, still chewing away at her donut. "You see Charlie over there by the window?"

I turned and saw an elderly man, his face sprinkled with liver spots, hunched over his morning paper. "He's ninety-six?"

"Ninety-seven," Betty said. "His hearing is bad, but he's sharp as a tack. Did you want to see Anne's room?"

Though slightly taken aback by the swift change in subject, I told Betty yes and explained that I was there to pick up a quilt Nora had given her.

"I know," Betty said with a sly grin. "*My* hearing is still good. Come along with me." She plopped the last of her donut in her mouth and happily licked her fingers.

Donna and Frank stayed behind while Betty took me down a brightly lit corridor to the right of the lobby's fireplace, her steps slow but sure. The grungy carpeting, stained walls, industrial furnishings, and other horrors I'd anticipated before my arrival were nowhere to be seen. It's not that I was naive. I knew that for some, such terrible places existed, but I was glad that Anne had lived among friends at Aspen Glen.

"Here we are," Betty said, stopping at room 114.

It occurred to me that the receptionist hadn't given me a key, and I was about to ask Betty how we'd get inside when she turned the knob and pushed the door open.

"Anne never locked her door," Betty said. "More proof that she wasn't stealing."

"It's like a studio apartment," I said. "There's even a microwave."

"They take good care of us here." Betty pointed to the bed. "There's Nora's quilt."

Folded neatly at the foot of the bed was a stunning ivory and red quilt, and on top of it, as if it had been casually tossed there, was Nora's miniature.

# CHAPTER 6

"You're sure you've never seen that painting in Mrs. Rightler's room before?" Chief Gilroy asked Betty.

Betty threw back her shoulders. "I would have remembered. Anne never had that in her room, and I've never seen it in anyone else's room."

"And I never have," Donna said.

Frank shook his head. "Never. I've never seen it anywhere."

After taking custody of the miniature, Gilroy had set up shop in the lobby, a place far more conducive to gently questioning the elderly residents. Several of the women had circled around Gilroy and were eagerly awaiting their turn to talk to him—almost as eagerly as they were eyeing the donut box. I did my best to keep from grinning, and I carefully kept just out of his line of sight.

*Face facts, he's one good-looking man*, I thought. Tall and trim, blue eyes, dark hair with touches of gray. Intelligent, thoughtful. Cowboy boots. So out of my league, but a girl could dream. Last month I'd started hiking the trail behind my house in hopes of shedding the extra twenty-five pounds I carried, but to no avail. Anyway, with just one coffee date and one lunch date under our belts—in an entire month—my hopes of romance were a pipe dream. He either liked me or didn't. Me with my dark hair, also with touches of gray, and that cowlick at the back of my head that was impossible to disguise. And truthfully, I was beginning to think his affections were lukewarm at best.

"Are those donuts for us?" one of the women asked Gilroy.

"Rachel brought those," Frank said. "Ask her."

"Who's Rachel?"

"I am," I said, giving a little wave. "The donuts are for everyone."

Half a dozen hands stretched out, and the donuts disappeared in a matter of seconds.

"Chief Gilroy, Rachel told me you intend to solve Anne's murder," Betty said.

"Did she?" Gilroy shot me a look over his shoulder, where I'd cleverly placed myself so he couldn't see me watching him.

A wisp of a woman, eighty years or older, squeezed herself onto the couch between Betty and Gilroy. "Was she murdered?" the woman asked.

"We haven't released that information yet," Gilroy said.

"That doesn't mean anything," Betty said, glaring at the interloper. "Like we told Rachel, Anne never took the stairs by herself. Someone pushed her. It's clear as can be."

Gilroy shot me another look, this one more scathing, before addressing Betty. "Finding that miniature will help the investigation, so thank you again."

"You're a police chief but you don't wear a uniform," Donna said, as if noticing for the first time that Gilroy was dressed in jeans and a dark olive barn coat.

"Some police chiefs do, some don't," Gilroy said,

getting to his feet. "I don't."

"Would you like some tea, Mr. Gilroy?" the interloper asked.

"Thank you, but no."

"Coffee?" a woman asked.

"No thanks, ma'am."

"We have the best coffee," Donna said. "Frank here will get it for you."

"I'm fine."

"We never get distinguished visitors," Betty said, imploring him with her eyes.

"Ah, well . . ."

Gilroy was rattled. I'd never seen him anywhere close to embarrassed before, but he was downright flustered and had no idea how to make his escape. I took pity on him, though not without enjoying his predicament. "Ladies, I think Chief Gilroy needs to get that painting back to the station. It's important he acts quickly if he's going to solve the case."

"Yes, yes," Betty said. "You look like a young man who means business, so you get on with it."

I chewed at my lower lip to keep from grinning, snatched Nora's quilt from a chair back, and hurried for the door.

"Very funny," Gilroy called out when I hit the parking lot.

I spun back. Unable to contain myself any longer, I burst into laughter.

He marched up to me. "You enjoyed that, did you?"

"I think they enjoyed it more."

He stepped close, bent his face to mine, and kissed me.

I sucked in my breath—not the most romantic of

responses—and Gilroy headed for his car. "Stay warm, Rachel. It started snowing."

For a moment I was rooted in place. I'd been oblivious to the snowflakes dancing in the air, the new membrane of snow on the asphalt parking lot. I turned back to see Gilroy getting in his police department SUV.

*Don't stand here like a statue.* I headed for my car, walking cautiously so I wouldn't slip and fall, which was just the sort of thing I'd do at such a moment. By the time I'd put the key in the ignition and checked my rearview mirror, Gilroy had left the parking lot.

"Oh, boy." I exhaled and raised a hand to my lips. Okay, so maybe he wasn't lukewarm, but why hadn't he said anything about his feelings? "Because he's James Gilroy," I said aloud.

Snow was beginning to collect on the windshield. I flicked on the wipers, brushing away the tiny, dry flakes, and headed out of the parking lot and onto the road. I felt like calling Julia—and immediately decided I wouldn't. What about Holly, then? No. This was too new, my thoughts too fragile. And if I told them now, this moment would be enshrined forevermore as the Kiss in the Snow, and I was far too old for that. Most of all, I feared overreacting. I'd closed myself off for so long after Brent left me that I had no sense of balance when it came to men. A man kissed me. So? He kissed me, that's all.

But he did kiss me. I felt a grin—a big, goofy grin—spread over my face as I pulled up to a stoplight on Main Street. A man in the crosswalk slowed and stared as he passed me by. Feeling as giddy as I'd felt in ages, I almost rolled down the window and shouted hello. Fortunately I had sense enough to restrain myself.

I had planned to visit the Front Range Historical Society on Orchard Street, just south of Main Street, and I intended to carry out my plan, kiss or no kiss. I'd promised Nora I would help her, and in a way I'd promised Anne the same. The miniature's mysterious reappearance in Anne's room gave me the perfect reason to talk to Kendra. She couldn't have heard yet that the police had recovered the painting.

By the time I turned onto Orchard Street, our little snowstorm had moved east and the sun was trying to break through the clouds. Julia had told me to look for a two-story red-sandstone house, not large, but grand looking in its own way, with an elaborate front entrance. I spotted it right away, pulled into a parking spot at the curb, and got out. The house had been built in the 1890s, Julia said, in the days when houses and businesses mingled in downtown Juniper Grove. And in fact, the house was hedged in by businesses—a restaurant on one side and a one-story office building on the other.

I made my way up the concrete walk and stood on the porch for a moment, reading the plaque outside the door that marked the house as only the seventh built in all of Juniper Grove.

A middle-aged woman, her hair in a high, loose bun, looked up from her desk as I entered, and I quickly glanced about the place, hoping to find Kendra.

"Can I help you?" the woman asked.

"I've never been here before," I said. Gesturing at the artifacts on display on the open shelves to my right, I added, "It's like a museum."

"It is—or it will be soon. That's the plan." The woman rose and began to conduct a hands-on mini-tour of the first floor, her fingers lovingly brushing over old school notebooks, an oil lamp, kitchen items, and framed embroidery samplers made by early settlers. "Of course there's more in the other rooms, but these are some of our smaller items."

"Anything related to St. Vrain?"

She seemed delighted I'd know the man's name. "It's almost impossible to come by anything contemporary. Of course, there are Bent's Fort and Fort St. Vrain, which his company built as trading posts, but small, personal items are rare." Her smile faded and her hands dropped to her sides. "We recently found a contemporary miniature portrait—a priceless artifact—but it was stolen."

"The police found the miniature this morning," I said.

"What?" She latched on to my arm. "Kendra!"

"That's why I'm here."

"Kendra!" The woman released my arm and wheeled around, disappearing through a door at the rear of the room.

I heard a muffled exchange of words and footsteps heavy on the wood floors. A moment later Kendra Wallace stormed through the door, her eyebrows arching in surprise when she recognized me. "What's this about the miniature?"

"It was found this morning. In the same condition it was in last night, I think." I'd examined it closely and taken a photo of it before calling Gilroy, and although my memory of what it had looked like last night was spotty, it didn't appear to have any new damage.

"That's wonderful!"

"It could have been damaged beyond repair," I said. To judge her reaction to the news, I decided to feed her information bit by bit. If she was genuinely surprised, I'd know it. Though judging by the way she'd raced up to me, she was not only surprised but also thrilled.

I heard what sounded like thumps on a staircase from somewhere at the back of the house, and a moment later Ben Wallace entered the room. "What's all the shouting about?"

"They found the miniature," Kendra replied. "Was it at Nora's?" she asked, turning back to me.

"No, at Aspen Glen, in Anne Rightler's room."

"Where?" Ben said.

"How did it get there?" Kendra asked.

"I know she took it," Ben said, giving his head a scratch. "We all knew, but . . ." His words trailed off.

"It's a mystery," I said, stating the obvious. "She didn't leave with the miniature, so how did it get to her room?"

"Where is it now?" Kendra said.

"With the police."

"Who found it?" Ben said.

"I went to pick up a quilt Nora had given Anne, and there it was."

"What a relief," Kendra said.

"But I don't understand how it got to Aspen Glen," Ben said, his brow knit in confusion.

"I don't care," Kendra said with a laugh. "It's back. That precious artifact is safe."

"No," Ben said, shaking his head. "Don't you see? That means someone else stole it, not Anne."

Seemingly bewildered by Ben's reaction, Kendra said, "Forget about who took it. We've got it back. Be happy."

"Ben has a point," I said. "Anne took it at first—did you all know she took things from the documents room?"

Ben grunted. "It was a problem for months. I begged Nora to do something about it."

"But I heard that whatever Anne took was always

returned," I said.

"I'm a historian," he replied. "The idea of historical documents disappearing, being mishandled in that way, concerned me. It was only a matter of time before something disappeared for good."

I decided the flames needed stoking. "So someone at Nora's Thanksgiving dinner took the miniature from Anne, and it ended up in her room at Aspen Glen—after she was murdered. That bothers me too, and I'm sure the police will care less about why it's back and more about who took it and who left it in Anne's room."

Kendra refused to have her mood dampened. "The most important thing is that the miniature was found, and from what you say, Rachel, it's undamaged."

I bit my tongue. I had an appreciation for history, but surely the most important thing was that Anne had lost her life.

"You're missing the point, Kendra," Ben said.

"No, I'm not. You're writing a dissertation. You don't need the originals of anything. I'm running the historical society, and for me, originals are all that matter."

"That dissertation will dictate whether this house becomes a museum. Their fates are intertwined."

"For the hundredth time, I know!"

Shocked by the intensity in her own voice, Kendra flinched. "I'm sorry, Rachel. This is a hot-spot subject for us."

Ben laid a hand on his wife's shoulder. "The past twenty-four hours have put us both on edge."

I gave them what I hoped was an understanding smile.

"Have you seen the society's collection?" Ben asked.

Behind us, the woman at the desk spoke up. "I showed

her, Mr. Wallace."

"Good, good. Kendra's worked tirelessly to bring all this together. If we get the city's approval, it becomes a museum."

"I think we're a shoo-in," Kendra said.

"This used to be the sitting room of this house," Ben went on. "The door behind Margaret leads to bedrooms, and that opening"—he gestured toward the other side of the room—"leads to what used to be the kitchen. Margaret, did you show Rachel the kitchen corner?"

"Just this room, Mr. Wallace."

"Before you go, you have to see this," Ben said. "Kendra pulled a coup when she reconstructed it. Follow me."

He was trying a little too hard to boost his wife's ego, but I reluctantly trailed after him. As we rounded the corner into the old kitchen, I heard the front door slam. Two seconds later a woman shouted, "They found that stupid painting! I told you he didn't steal it! Now do you believe me?"

Ben halted and pivoted back. "Sheila?"

He swung around me and strode for the door. I followed, but where the kitchen opening met the sitting room, I stopped and looked toward the front door.

Sheila Larson's expression changed from defiance to confusion in the blink of an eye when she saw me. "Rachel?"

Kendra, her arms across her chest and her foot tapping like an impatient parent, glared back at Sheila. "I know they found it, but we still don't know who stole it, do we?"

# CHAPTER 7

Before heading home for dinner and an after-dinner meeting of the Juniper Grove Mystery Gang, I decided to make a stop at Nora's house. She'd probably heard from Gilroy about the miniature, but I wanted more information on her Thanksgiving guests, and I wanted to see the cellar stairs for myself.

Questions about the miniature were still running themselves over in my mind. As soon as I settled on a possible explanation for why it was stolen or how it traveled from Anne's pocket to her room at Aspen Glen, more questions and competing theories appeared. On the other hand, Kendra's and Sheila's confrontation at the Historical Society could mean only one thing: Kendra had accused Dominic of stealing the miniature. And Kendra was right. Just because the painting had been found didn't mean that Dominic hadn't taken it. Someone at Nora's Thanksgiving dinner had.

I called Nora to let her know I was coming and asked her if she'd heard about the miniature. She had. Gilroy had taken it to her after leaving Aspen Glen. When I arrived, she was still riding high on the painting's discovery and answered my knock on her door with a wide grin on her face. I understood her relief, but I was disturbed by her and her friends' focus on this little painting. Anne Rightler had lost her life because of it. Couldn't they see that? I almost wished the miniature had never been found. Or discovered among Nora's things in the first place.

"Do you mind if I take a look at the cellar steps?" I asked, draping my coat over the back of an armchair.

"Not at all. Look at anything you need to."

Nora led me down the hallway, stopping at the first door on the right. "This is the restroom. I reminded Anne it was the first door on her right arm—like this." She patted her own right arm, reenacting her conversation.

"Was the door open?"

"Yes, just like it is now."

"And the cellar door?"

Nora walked ten more feet, stopped, and pointed to her right. "Here. The last door in the hall. It's closed, just like it was at Thanksgiving."

The doors were indistinguishable from each other and the two doors on the left. All four were white, with recessed panels and brass doorknobs. "Do you know if it was open when Kendra found Anne?"

"She said it was open. I heard her tell Gilroy."

I looked to the ceiling. "I remember these two light fixtures being on."

"I knew people would be using the restroom, and one switch turns both lights on."

With a slight flutter of nerves, I opened the cellar door and gazed down the steps. Surprisingly, there was no landing at the top of the stairs. Anyone misjudging the first step would almost certainly tumble down the entire staircase. There was a banister on the left, but in a fall it would have been useless to an elderly person with little upper body strength. At the bottom of the flight of stairs, the spot where Anne had hit the concrete floor was marked with a large red-brown stain.

"Nora, these steps are dangerous," I said.

"That's why I keep the door shut."

"Can you lock it?" I inspected the doorknob's back plate for a keyhole.

"No, but I could have a locksmith come out."

"You could have him put a simple latch on the door and jamb," I said, touching the door frame. "Up here, so someone has to work at unlatching it."

"That's an idea."

I gave the steps a last look and shut the door slowly, studying the shadows it made as it closed. "I'd be afraid to use those stairs, Nora. One misstep and I'd fall down the entire flight. But your overhead lights are bright, and even when the door is open barely enough for a person to pass through it, the stairs are clearly visible. You can't mistake this door for the restroom door or a bedroom door."

Nora nodded. "I don't need a police report or medical examiner's report. There's no doubt in my mind that Anne was pushed."

"I agree." I didn't mention that Officer Underhill had told Holly about backward hand prints on Anne's arms, indicating that she had been grabbed from behind. That was Gilroy's domain, and besides, I didn't want to get Underhill in trouble. If Gilroy discovered his officer was talking about the case at the bakery, he'd flip. "And this door is at the far end of the hall. You can't see it from the living room unless you're actually standing where the hall and living room meet. Do you mind if I take a look around?"

"By all means. What are you looking for?"

"I'd like to know how that miniature got out of the house."

"It wasn't here Thanksgiving night," Nora said with the certainty that comes from authority, merited or not. She adjusted her glasses with her fingertips and marched back up the hall. Back in the living room, she spread her arms wide, emphasizing the far-flung reaches of the room. "The police searched every corner of every room. They started their search while you were still here, but they went on long after. They lifted up lamps and opened drawers, they looked in bookcases. The kitchen, the dining room, the restrooms, the documents room, the bedrooms. They were lifting up mattresses, for goodness' sake."

"But the police searched every person who left your house. Their coats and even their clothes."

"Ben was especially upset. He thought I should take his word that he didn't steal it. Not on your life."

I told Nora about the confrontation between Kendra and Sheila. She didn't seem surprised. "Do you think Dominic would take the miniature?" I asked.

"Out of envy, yes." Nora appeared pained by the thought. She sat down and gestured for me to do the same. "I knew Dominic would be upset that I didn't let him insure the painting, but I wanted an art specialist. I needed it to be insured for the proper amount and with the proper documentation, and Dominic is a money man, not an art man."

"But I understand he insures virtually everything else in the documents room."

"Nothing else up there is worth as much. I let him insure the rest because that's how he makes much of his living. Have you heard of cross-selling?"

I said I hadn't.

"It's when a financial adviser at a bank—that's what Dominic is—sells other products, like bank accounts, life insurance, or financial investments. There's nothing wrong with it, technically, but the pressure to do it, just to keep your job, can be enormous. On top of that, Dominic makes a commission with each referral—like insuring new discoveries in my documents room. He makes his living by cross-selling *me*." Her tone carried the sadness she no doubt felt. Dominic made his living by convincing her to let him handle all her financial needs. Now I understood what Paige had said on Thanksgiving about Nora letting Dominic control her money way too much. Though how Paige, a caterer, would know that rather personal information was a puzzle. Maybe the girl was simply more observant than most.

"So that's why Dominic was so angry yesterday about Ben and Kendra's insurer," I said.

"An insurer unrelated to the company Dominic uses. With my blessing."

"He lost money."

"And I think he and Sheila are having financial troubles."

"Do you suspect Dominic more than the others?"

"I suspect them all equally."

"Why would Kendra or Ben steal the miniature?"

"The same reason as Dominic. Money. Kendra's obsessed with turning the Historical Society into a museum."

"I thought you approved of that."

"I do! But it's all she ever talks about. Every time she finds a new document, she says, 'Can we donate this to the museum?' It's the same thing with Ben, only he wants to use the documents for his dissertation. That's *his* obsession. He wants a full professorship, and the only way he's going to do that is by using my undiscovered documents for his dissertation. 'Shake Colorado history to its foundations,' he likes to say. He's completely full of himself, of course."

"How many documents do you have up there?"

"Hundreds. Diaries, legal documents, letters. Anything you can imagine. My great-grandfather collected historical documents related to Colorado, and his father even met St. Vrain once. Several generations' worth of acquisitions came my way. Fifty years ago, no one else in the family was interested in any of it, so my husband and I took it. We thought we'd get around to sorting through it, but we never did. Then he died six years ago."

"I'm sorry."

"He was a good man," she said, her voice wavering for the space of those few words. "And I'm well taken care of. Now, where was I? Kendra. She has to verify each discovery. Is it genuine? That's her department. Finding the miniature was a coup for her, and I'm sure she's looking for another coup."

"So how would stealing the miniature benefit her or Ben? They could never display it in the museum."

"They could *sell* it, Rachel. Kendra wants to turn several rooms in the society's house into re-creations. Right now she's consumed by re-creating an old kitchen. She can restore some things, but others she'll have to buy."

"Did you plan to donate the miniature to the Historical Society?"

"Kendra thinks I did. She and the others think it's a done deal, but I haven't decided yet."

"How about Sheila? Would she have taken the

miniature?"

"Sheila wants Dominic to succeed. Her fate is tethered to his."

But Sheila was far too timid to steal an expensive historical artifact, I thought. Wasn't that the stuff of cat burglars? The woman I met on Thanksgiving was more upset than Nora when Dominic and Ben began to argue. She struck me as someone who avoided conflict at all cost. I recalled her sitting silently on the couch after Anne's body was found, twisting her red hair in her fingers, refusing Underhill's attempts at comfort. And I'd heard pleasure in her voice when she told Kendra that the painting had been found, thus vindicating Dominic, at least in her own mind. Then again, she may have suspected her husband of the theft, and it wasn't pleasure I'd heard when she spoke to Kendra, it was relief.

"Nora, do you think Kendra accused Dominic to his face? Or did she speak only to Sheila?"

"Kendra knew that anything she said to Sheila would get back to Dominic, and she liked to, well, torment her that way. I think that's the appropriate word."

"Sheila didn't fight back?"

"Sheila lacks gumption." Nora's expression became somber. "All these people in my house—for Thanksgiving, of all holidays—none of them are friends, really. They take advantage of me. And except for Sheila, they're not very kind. I think I'll do something different for Christmas."

"That sounds like a very good idea."

"But Anne won't be here. She *was* a friend, and how she loved Christmas."

Nora met my eyes briefly, then looked away, and finally I glimpsed the sadness I considered the natural reaction. This was a woman who hid her emotions, I thought. She lived alone, she felt vulnerable, and she thought it best to keep cool. Even in mentioning her late husband, Nora had maintained an even keel. Only her voice, faltering for an instant, had betrayed her.

"And to think she was killed because an ugly little portrait is worth a lot of money," Nora said.

"I've been thinking that the theft may not be why Anne was killed."

"But it has to be."

"Why kill her and then take the painting? Why not take the painting on another night? They all would have had ample opportunity, wouldn't they?"

"They're here all the time. Kendra especially."

"So why ruin their chance at a clean getaway by murdering someone and ensuring that the police would show up and search them and the house?"

Her shoulders slumped and she sank deeper into the couch. "We still haven't solved the mystery of how the painting left my house, have we?"

In frustration, I threw my hands up. "I don't see how it's possible. If they hadn't scoured the shrubs and lawn, maybe. But they did."

"They searched and patted down every person who walked out my door, you included. Has anyone ever had a Thanksgiving like that?"

"Underhill even went through Julia's purse."

"And Kendra's," Nora said with a chuckle. "They didn't miss a thing."

Again I went over the events in my mind, retracing my steps and what I could recall of others' movements. Gilroy and Underhill had continued to search the house and grounds after Julia and I left, but that didn't matter in my calculations. By then the miniature had vanished. And then it hit me. "Oh yes, they did miss something." I sprang from the couch.

"Rachel?"

"I have to talk to Gilroy right now," I said, racing for the door. "I'll call you, Nora."

# CHAPTER 8

I'd never known the police station to be locked, but now, when I desperately needed to talk to Gilroy, it was. I yanked on the door and then rapped on the glass. Nothing. Where were they? I knew Gilroy's policy was to have a man at the station at all times until midnight. Underhill had grumbled about the policy on more than one occasion. I had a sneaking suspicion it was Officer Underhill's turn to watch the desk, and he'd decided to run some errands instead. Or take a nap in the back.

I pulled my phone from my jeans pocket and dialed the station's number. Through the door I could hear the desk phone ring, but no one appeared from the back rooms to answer it. If Underhill was napping in Gilroy's office—or in a cell—he was choosing to ignore the phone.

Back in my car, I considered my next step. Should I warn Paige? Give her a chance to turn herself in so Gilroy would go easy on her? There was only one way that miniature could have left the house, and that was in Paige's leftovers. I pictured how she did it—protecting the painting in plastic wrap, hiding it in the large container of mashed potatoes she took with her. So large I'd wondered if she'd left any for the rest of us. If I hadn't been so focused on the mashed potatoes, I might have paid more attention to the fact that Gilroy and Underhill hadn't searched any of the leftovers, mine included.

I looked for Calloway Catering on my phone, found an apartment address a block north of downtown, and headed out. Paige had packed up everyone's leftovers in Nora's kitchen. No one else had touched them. But my instincts were telling me Paige hadn't killed Anne, and maybe she hadn't even taken the miniature from the elderly woman's pocket. Paige was an unusually observant girl. She knew all about the people she served at Nora's dinners. Their financial woes, their troubles, their jealousies. No, my guess was that she'd seen someone take the miniature from Anne and hide it in the house. And then, before the police arrived, she'd taken it herself, hiding it where no one would look.

Was Nora's caterer a brazen thief? I recalled Anne's words at Thanksgiving—"I know exactly who the thief is"—and the sound of shattering glass that came next. And I remembered Paige's disdain for the Wallaces' and Larsons' money troubles because both couples had more than most. Paige was a thief, that I could believe, but she was no murderer. That was of little comfort, because if I was right in thinking Paige wasn't the killer, she probably knew who the killer was.

I pulled up to her two-story apartment building, parked, and sped for the main door, barreling ahead so I wouldn't change my mind and leave it up to Gilroy. Paige was too young to have her life ruined by one foolish moment.

As I took the stairs to Paige's apartment on the second floor, I rehearsed what I'd say to her, but by the time I reached her door, I'd given up. There were no magic words. She would listen or she wouldn't. I reached up to knock on the door but stopped cold.

It was open a crack, and I could hear a radio or television playing inside. "Paige?" I rapped my knuckles on the door and pushed on it, opening it a few more inches. "Paige, are you here? It's Rachel Stowe."

I pushed the door wider. The smell of overheated metal was coming from a pot on the small kitchen stove, an oven light was on, and vegetables were strewn over the kitchen island. *Wrong*.

I stepped inside the door and called out again. There was a carving knife on the floor at the end of the island, and in the tiny living room, an ottoman had been overturned.

"Paige, where are you?"

I strode to the TV and switched it off. When I turned back around, I saw her on the floor.

My first impulse was to dive for the door, but half a second later I realized Paige's killer had to be long gone.

I turned off the stove top and oven, and I knocked the screaming-hot pot off its burner with a quick elbow jab. Another couple minutes and the pot would have been welded to the range.

Paige had been strangled. At least that's what I suspected when I first saw her. And when I worked up the courage to glance back at her, my suspicion was confirmed. I could see the ligature marks on her neck. I called the police station on my cell, hoping someone would be there to answer my call. Underhill was. I made a snide remark about him waking up from a nap, gave him Paige's address, and then hung up.

To keep one of Paige's neighbors from walking in on her, I pushed the apartment door shut, again using my elbow. There were no signs of a break-in at the door. No splintered wood or kick marks. Paige had trusted her killer.

I inspected the kitchen, being careful not to touch or step on any evidence, and found Paige's Thanksgiving container in a trash bin by the refrigerator. The lid was gone, and so were half the mashed potatoes. But I could see a distinct oval-shaped impression in the potatoes that remained, and next to the container was what looked like bunched-up plastic wrap.

My gaze wandered about Paige's apartment, over the thrift-store coffee table, the basic-beige walls, the framed art print from the Denver Museum above the tiny bookcase, the twin-sized bed in a corner off the living room. And Paige's body at the foot of the bed. I looked away from her. It was a dorm room, not a home. She couldn't have had much money. But everyone starting a business made sacrifices. Had Paige grown tired of scrimping and saving, serving people who owned far more than she did? I moved back toward the door and stood next to the half-wall separating the kitchen from the bedroom.

Gilroy entered without a knock, his eyes shooting to mine. "Are you all right?"

Suddenly I couldn't speak. I nodded.

Underhill, his camera strap around his neck, sidestepped around us into the living room and then made a sharp pivot to his right. "Here, Chief."

Gilroy joined Underhill, and I looked around for a place to sit. Having gotten over the initial shock of seeing Paige, my legs had grown wobbly.

A moment later Gilroy leaned across the half-wall, handed me a ring full of keys, and told me to sit in the police SUV. He didn't have to ask twice.

Sitting in the back seat of the SUV, I could feel the cold vinyl on my back, cutting right through my coat. I wrapped my arms around myself. The coroner arrived in five minutes, and five minutes after that, Gilroy came out to the SUV.

"Are you sure you're all right?" he asked, climbing into the front and sitting sideways.

"I'm okay. Just tired all of a sudden."

"That's understandable. I need to go back in, but before I do, I have to ask you some questions."

"That's fine."

"First, what you were doing here?" The look he gave me wasn't quite the look of disapproval I'd grown used to, but neither was it neutral. There I was at another murder scene. What on earth was I up to now?

"I figured out how the miniature got out of Nora's house, and I guess . . ." I paused. Underhill could be lazy at times, but he wasn't a bad cop, and I didn't want to get him in trouble by telling Gilroy I'd tried to reach him at the station. "I guess I wanted to convince Paige to tell you she'd taken it and maybe . . . you know, tell you she did it before you found out so maybe . . ."

Gilroy was frowning. I couldn't blame him. I was babbling.

"Let's back up," he said. "How did the miniature get out of the house?"

"In Paige's container of leftover mashed potatoes."

His frown doubled.

"She covered it in plastic wrap and stuck it in the middle of the mashed potatoes. If you look in her kitchen trash bin, you can still see the container and the impression the miniature made in it, and the discarded plastic wrap next to the container. I didn't touch anything, so don't look at me like that."

"Stay here."

Gilroy raced back into the apartment building, no doubt to check the trash bin. Underhill wasn't a bad cop, but he wasn't an especially talented one, either. A few minutes later Gilroy came back out, an evidence bag in his hand. He stored the bag in the SUV's cargo area and then hoisted himself back into the front seat. Before I could say anything, Underhill got into the passenger seat, his camera swinging at his neck.

"Did you touch anything else?" Underhill said.

"All I touched was the doorknob and the switches for the oven and range top. They were both on when I got here. I pushed the hot pot off the burner with my elbow."

"You just walked in?" Underhill asked.

He was annoyed with me, thinking I'd deliberately shown him up. "The door was open a crack. I heard the TV on, and something seemed wrong. Then I smelled the burning pot. I knew what it was because I've left boiling water on the stove too long."

Gilroy threw his arm over the seat back and angled in his seat to face me. "Did anyone else know you were coming here?"

"No one. I was at Nora's house, but I left without telling her where I was going. I called the station two minutes after walking into Paige's apartment."

"Why didn't you call the station before you drove out here? You suspected Miss Calloway of stealing an expensive painting and you thought it was a good idea to waltz out here on your own?"

"I was hardly waltzing."

"She's *dead*, Rachel. Someone killed her—and not that long ago."

"Um . . ." Underhill took off his hat, scratched his head,

and looked from Gilroy to me. "I saw the caller ID when I got back. That was your cell phone number, wasn't it?"

"Yeah."

"Sorry," Underhill said.

"About what?" Gilroy asked, regarding Underhill suspiciously.

"I left the station to run an errand. I guess Miss Stowe called while I was out. Before she got here, I mean."

I couldn't believe he had fessed up. Maybe he was a better man than I gave him credit for. "That's okay," I said.

"No, it's not okay," Gilroy said flatly. "We'll talk about this later, Underhill."

"Right." Underhill faced front.

Gilroy shut his eyes and ran a hand over his face. The job's long hours were taking a toll on him. When he opened his eyes, for the briefest of moments he gave me a look so tender it melted my heart.

Then he shifted back to chief mode. "Underhill, take charge of the scene."

"Yes, Chief." Underhill slid down from his seat and trudged back into the apartment building.

I was about to come to Underhill's defense, pointing out that they were both working insane hours, when Gilroy said, "Did you see anyone when you drove up? Or anyone inside the building?"

"No one."

"Did you discuss the miniature with anyone after you left Aspen Glen?"

I told him about my visit to the Historical Society and Sheila's sudden appearance there. "Ben and Kendra were surprised the miniature had been found, but happy. Both of them would have job and money troubles if something happened to that painting. I think Kendra accused Dominic of taking it at Thanksgiving, but not to his face. She told Sheila instead. Nora says Kendra likes to tweak Sheila's nose."

Out the windshield, I saw a black sedan park two cars in front of Gilroy's SUV. Dominic Larson emerged from the driver's side. He walked slowly toward Paige's apartment building, looking as though he might change his mind and run for his car at any moment. For such a tall, commanding man, he took oddly small and uncertain steps. When the coroner's assistants came out of the building wheeling Paige's body, he stopped dead in his tracks.

Gilroy got out and walked over to him, and I popped open the back door so I could catch what they were saying.

"Chief Gilroy, what happened?"

"I'm afraid one of the residents has died. Were you here to see someone?"

"Yes, Paige Calloway."

"I'm sorry to have to tell you, but Miss Calloway is dead."

Dominic moaned. Either he was a very good actor or he was genuinely upset. "What happened?"

"Did she know you were coming?"

"We had an appointment. Paige is a caterer. My wife and I are planning an anniversary party next month."

As I listened to Dominic and Gilroy, I wondered if Dominic was in on the theft and had shown up for his cut—or for the prize miniature itself. According to Nora, he needed the money, though I could imagine him stealing the painting just to spite Kendra and Ben. And good acting or not, I found it hard to believe that his emotions over Paige's death were genuine. Had Dominic been here earlier, killed

Paige, and come back just for show?

# CHAPTER 9

"I'll bring the coffee, you two go sit," I said, waving Julia and Holly out of my kitchen.

"Where do you keep the notepads?" Holly asked.

"Last drawer on the right. Grab some pens too."

After driving home from Paige's apartment building, I'd scarfed the entire cream puff I'd bought at Holly's Sweets. No dinner, just a huge cream puff. I felt full, a little sloppy, and good. I'd been looking forward to this meeting of the Juniper Grove Mystery Gang—so christened by Holly—all day, especially after finding Paige's body. It was the first thing I said when Julia and Holly rang my doorbell. "Paige Calloway is dead, and we need to find out why."

Not that I'd forgotten Anne, but the two murders were connected, I was sure.

I set the cups, a carton of half-and-half, and a ceramic coffeepot on a tray and carried it into the living room. "Help yourselves." I poked the logs in my fireplace, stoking the fire, then poured myself a cup and sank into my comfy couch.

"Was it horrible?" Holly said.

"It was more sad than anything," I replied, taking a sip of coffee.

"She was so young," Julia said.

"I don't understand why she felt she needed to steal that painting," I said. "She was a talented cook, judging by those leftovers we had last night."

"Those leftovers were good for more than eating," Julia said with a wry smile. "I can't believe the painting escaped in a plastic container of mashed potatoes. How did Paige ever think of it?"

"I'm not sure she did," I said. "I don't think she was in it alone. She had no connections to the historical art world, and so she had no way to sell the painting—a very special painting with a niche market. All the others have connections."

"You said Dominic Larson showed up at her apartment while you were there?" Holly said.

I nodded. "Supposedly to meet with Paige about catering his anniversary party next month."

"Suspicious timing."

"It should be easy enough to find out if he really did have an appointment," I said. "Paige must have an appointment book for her business."

"I wonder . . ." Holly drew her long, dark ponytail over her shoulder and absentmindedly brushed it with her fingers. "How did the painting go from Paige's apartment to Anne's room? Obviously Anne didn't take it there. Who did? And why? Why not leave it with Nora Barberton? It's almost as if whoever did it thought the painting belonged with Anne's things."

"I should take a look at her room again," I said.

"I wonder if the person who put the miniature in Anne's room killed Paige to get it," Julia said. "I know you said Paige was killed hours later, Rachel, but the killer could have returned to her apartment."

"She knew her killer," I said. "That settles it. Tomorrow I'm going back to Aspen Glen. That miniature didn't walk itself to Anne's room. Someone took it there, and one of the residents had to have seen who."

"I'm going with you," Julia said. "Maybe they'll be more willing to talk to an older person."

"They were more than willing to talk to Gilroy," I said, "and he's not quite a senior." I laughed, recalling how perilously close he'd come to blushing, and then recounted the scene for Julia and Holly.

"I don't think I've ever seen him ruffled," Holly said.

"Oh, he was ruffled," I said. I took a long, slow sip of coffee. The words were on the tip of my tongue—*he kissed me*—and I wanted to wash them down. Part of me thought the magic of it all would vanish if I said the words aloud. I *liked* James Gilroy. A lot. And for some strange reason, he seemed to like me. Weird cowlick, pointy chin, flabby tummy, and all. I gave in. "He kissed me."

"Gilroy?" Julia said. She shot forward on the couch and set her cup so roughly on the table that coffee sloshed over the side.

Holly whooped. "When? When did this happen?"

"This morning, after we left Aspen Glen."

"When were you going to tell us?" Julia said.

"I'm telling you now."

"Outside or inside the home?" Holly asked.

I laughed. "Does it make a difference? Outside in the parking lot. It was snowing."

"Aww," Julia said.

"It was fate—you finding that painting," Holly said. "Totally a God thing. And then you and Gilroy met again at Paige's apartment building. Amazing. Do you think he was upset you found out how the painting disappeared from Nora Barberton's house before he did?"

"He's so tired I don't know how he can find his own hands. I think he was more upset that I put myself in danger."

"Aww."

"Julia, if you make that sound again, we're changing subjects."

"I can't help it."

"I figured," Holly said. "Chief Gilroy would never be petty. He's a good man."

"So you've told me on many occasions," I said.

"As I have," Julia said, a huge grin filling her face. She looked like she was about to squeal with delight. "I'm so happy for you I can hardly stand it!"

"Julia, it was just a kiss," I said. "I don't know what, if anything, will come of it." In truth, I was tempering my reaction more than hers. Believing that a kiss held any promise for the future would leave me vulnerable, and I'd spent too many years post-Brent feeling vulnerable to willingly put myself in that position again.

Thankfully, Julia and Holly dropped all the questions that must have been whirling about their heads, and Holly suggested we get back to the job at hand: considering suspects and motivations in both Anne's and Paige's murders.

"I'm pretty sure we can rule out Paige as a suspect in Anne's murder," I said. "The other four are much more likely."

"What about Nora?" Holly asked.

Julia's jaw dropped. "Never, ever. I've known her for more than thirty years, and it's not possible." She was adamant in her friend's defense.

Holly spoke in a gentle voice. "I doubt she killed anyone, but to be fair, we should examine the facts and consider the possibility. From what you and Rachel have told me about Thanksgiving dinner, you don't know exactly when Anne disappeared or who was with her at the time. Or who followed her down the hall or where anyone was when you were with Paige in the kitchen."

"That's true," I said. I got up to poke the fire again. The logs crackled and flames rose from between them, generating new warmth. "Julia was upstairs looking for ointment and a Band-Aid for Paige's finger, and I was with Paige in the kitchen. When Julia came downstairs, Anne was telling everyone she knew who this thief was. Then Julia gave Paige the Band-Aid, and we went into the living room. By then, Anne was gone."

Julia nodded her agreement with my recitation of the events. "And Nora said that Anne asked to use the restroom."

"And she had to be reminded where it was," I said. "Then it seems everyone lost track of time *and* Anne. You were in the kitchen for what, Julia? Ten minutes, maybe?"

"Something like that."

I sat forward, my thoughts tumbling with images of the evening. "I remember now. When I returned to the living room after talking to Paige, the Larsons had moved to a different couch. There were two couches facing each other. When I got up to talk to Nora, the Larsons were on one couch and the Wallaces were with Nora. I asked to talk privately to Nora, so the Wallaces left. But then, when I came back to Julia—"

"After leaving me with Dominic and telling him I wanted wine," Julia said.

"Sorry. So when I came back, the Larsons were sitting

on the opposite couch. Both of them had moved."

"Dominic was getting wine in the kitchen," Julia said.

"He was a little too eager to get us wine, don't you think?"

"Now that I look back."

"I see why Dominic moved, maybe, but why did Sheila?" I asked, looking from Holly to Julia.

Holly tore a sheet of paper off her notepad, folded it twice, and then tore the sheet into four rectangles. Scooting to the edge of her seat, she pushed the coffee tray aside, penned initials on the rectangles, and positioned them on the coffee table. "Kendra and Ben, Dominic and Sheila," she said, pointing at the rectangles. "Let's go through this again."

"But is it important that they changed seats?" Julia asked.

"I think it's important that Sheila changed her seat," I answered.

"I do too," Holly said. "Something's not right here."

The three of us went over the sequence of events again, in as much detail as Julia and I could remember, but no matter which way we looked at it, Sheila's change of seats made no sense. About the time Dominic went to get wine for Julia, but before the Wallaces left me to talk privately with Nora, Sheila changed couches. Was it as simple as Sheila wanting a change of view? Maybe. But I didn't think so.

"We need to talk to Sheila," I said. "Nora told me she works at home. If I could find—"

"I could talk to her," Holly interrupted. "Tomorrow at the bakery. She comes in every Saturday morning about nine o'clock to pick up apple strudel for Sunday breakfast."

"That won't work," Julia said. "You can't introduce

yourself and say, 'I heard you were at a house where a woman was murdered. Mind telling me why you changed seats?'"

"There are always ways when pastry is involved," Holly said.

"Why don't I wait for her outside the bakery, then go inside when she comes?" I said.

"And what?" Julia said. "Block the door while Holly corners her? You ladies are not thinking this through."

"Do you have a better idea?" Holly said.

Julia pursed her lips, considering the question. "Let me try. I've met the Larsons at other dinners. I'll come up with a good reason to run into her and talk about the party."

"In public," I warned. "The only reason I can think of for Sheila to have changed seats was that she got up to follow Anne down the hall, and when she came back, she mistakenly took another seat."

"She wasn't thinking straight after shoving Anne down the stairs," Holly added. "I think you should take Rachel with you."

"She won't talk to Rachel," Julia said.

"I'll stay out of sight," I said. "You can run into her outside the bakery while I sit in my car. I'll drive."

Julia rolled her eyes. "I guess it's a plan. I still think you're making way too much of this. As if people don't move around at dinner parties. She could have had an uncomfortable cushion."

Holly yawned, stretched, and stood. "Ladies, I need to go."

"It's almost past your bedtime," I said.

"Be outside the bakery before nine tomorrow," she said, heading for the door. "Sometimes Sheila gets there a little early. Sometimes a little late too, but always around nine."

"I'm looking forward to this," Julia said, trailing after Holly. "It's like being a spy. I'll have to come up with a game plan."

I watched as Holly headed down my porch steps and made her way across the street to her house. "I can't imagine getting up at four in the morning six days a week. Can you?"

"The life of a baker," Julia replied. She stood still, her hand on my door. "I have a serious question, Rachel. Do you really like Gilroy?"

I didn't hesitate. "Yes."

Surprised that I hadn't tap-danced around the question as I usually did, Julia's eyebrows arched. "Good for you. I knew the minute you first looked at him, and he at you."

"Go home."

To my surprise, Julia hugged me. She was a nudged, not a hugger. I laughed and shooed her out the door.

# CHAPTER 10

I'd been writing in my upstairs office, working on my latest mystery novel, for an hour when I got a call from Nora. She claimed she'd discovered more thefts from her documents room and I needed to see the evidence for myself. When I suggested she call the police, she said it was a matter for me, not the police, and that the evidence was of a flimsy nature. "Flimsy" was her word.

But she piqued my interest, and I was wide awake again after writing, so I went. After I looked at her evidence, I could ask her to tell me in more detail what she remembered about everyone's whereabouts. Though I wasn't hopeful she'd recall anything more than she already had, I was game to look at her living room again. I could put myself where Sheila sat when she changed couches and perhaps see what she had seen.

Before I had a chance to knock at her door, Nora met me and ushered me inside. "I'm beyond upset," she said, instructing me to follow her up the stairs to the documents room. "I found out by pure chance."

She flicked on the room's lights, marched for the desk, and grabbed two stapled printouts that were on her computer keyboard. She shook them as though they were naughty children and then laid them side by side on the desk, facing me. "Look at this. I've been a fool."

I drew closer. As far as I could see, the first pages were two identical numbered lists of documents and artifacts, cataloged by Kendra Wallace. "What am I supposed to see?"

Nora pointed at the first printout. "This is Kendra's list. Now look at the other list." She tapped the second printout. "This one's mine. I kept it in a dresser drawer in my bedroom. They're supposed to be exact." She pointed at item 22, first on Kendra's list, then on hers.

"They're different," I said. On Nora's list, item 22 was an Arapaho ledger drawing made circa 1890, but on Kendra's list it was a photograph of a portrait of Charles Bent, then the governor of New Mexico Territory.

"Every other item on Kendra's list is the same, until you get to the very bottom, where there's a new item number 34 to replace the missing item 22. Item 34 is the first on the second page in my list."

"Is this Arapaho ledger drawing in your documents room?"

Nora tugged at her scarf, squeezed her hands together, wrung them, and then breathed, "No. It's gone. First Anne is killed, then Paige, and now . . ."

"You heard about Paige?"

"Chief Gilroy told me. I can't bear to think about it."

I thought it best not to mention that I had found her. Gilroy probably hadn't. I looked again at Nora's printout. From what I'd read, ledger drawings were worth a lot of money. I rather artlessly asked Nora if she'd priced the drawing.

"It's worth over seven hundred dollars, Rachel."

I took off my coat and laid it on a small table near the door, one of the few bare spots in the room. "Is it insured?"

"Yes, but that's not the point." She flipped through both stapled lists until she came to the third page on each. "Item 13, a letter from St. Vrain's wife. It's missing from Kendra's list and it's not in the documents room."

I glanced about the room, noting the floor-to-ceiling bookshelves at one end, brimming with document boxes, notebooks, and loose papers, and next to that, white cabinets, also stuffed to the gills—except for where the miniature of St. Vrain had sat. "Are you sure these things are missing? Could they have been moved? After all, Kendra's cataloging everything. She must have to shuffle things around, put them in new locations."

Nora was restlessly pacing, rubbing her forehead. "Maybe. Maybe. Do you think so?"

"Nora, sit down. You'll make yourself sick." I motioned for her to sit the only place available, the office chair.

"That doesn't explain the differences in the list," she said, sinking into the chair. She fidgeted and it creaked.

"I think you should take these lists to Chief Gilroy."

She looked up at me, tears welling in her eyes. "If I can't remember what was in this room, and *where* it was, how can he help me?"

"You have the lists."

"But I could be wrong. Maybe Kendra asked to sell those things to finance her work and I can't remember."

A shock ran through me. *Lord, no*. "Nora, are you having trouble remembering things?"

She looked away. "It only just started. Alzheimer's. It comes and goes, but most of the time I'm the same as I ever was. I'll be fine for a couple years, and a couple years after that if I hire help. That's what they tell me." She turned back, entreating me. "Only a few friends know. Please don't tell anyone."

I laid a hand on her shoulder. "I won't. I promise."

She rose from her chair and cleared her throat. "Back to business."

I remembered Nora talking to me about her husband, briefly, and about Anne, again briefly. I was sure she hid her emotions so she wouldn't feel vulnerable, but I'd misjudged her. She hid them—beat them down—only when they threatened to overwhelm her. Because she had to get on with her life. She needed *gumption*. There was no other way. "Are you going to ask Kendra about the discrepancies?"

"I'm not sure. Tell me how Kendra could do this to me. That's what I'd like to know."

"Would you like me to talk to Kendra? There could be a very good explanation."

She straightened her spine and peered at me over the tops of her glasses, her eyes twinkling. Nora the Strong was back. "Can you imagine there's an explanation for those discrepancies that doesn't involve stealing?"

"Honestly? No. But that's why you should talk to the police."

She shook her head. "Do you know what they'd tell me? Prove it. And I can't, not now. But I need to know if Kendra is stealing from me. And Ben! They're up here all the time, and I never watch them. I trusted them."

"Then let me talk to Kendra. Don't confront her. And Nora . . ." I waited until she ceased fiddling with her scarf and looked me in the eyes. "Don't assume she's stealing. You'll never be able to take an accusation like that back."

"I won't say a word."

I wasn't convinced. Nora was impulsive and strong,

and those traits, along with the beginnings of memory loss, didn't bode well for her keeping her promise.

"What do I do in the meantime, Rachel? Kendra and Ben are supposed to be here tomorrow. I can't leave them alone in this room."

"When are they coming?"

"Nine o'clock."

"Tell them whatever you need to, but don't let them in before ten. Text them."

Nora brightened. "I have their numbers. I won't have to speak to them until you're here."

"If I can, I'll bring Julia." I grabbed my coat, hoping it would signal my need to leave.

"Oh, I love Julia. Our husbands use to fish together, did you know that? Of course, her husband was a real stinker." She flipped the light switch and made her way to the top of the stairs, but before descending, she turned back to me, winking. "I can say that because Julia used to say worse."

"I know about George Foster," I said with a chuckle.

"Julia told me. It's why I'm asking you to help me."

Back in the living room, I remembered that I wanted to sit where Sheila Larson had sat when she'd changed positions, useless though that probably was. I told Nora what I was up to and then sat on the leftmost cushion of the three-seat couch, the exact spot where Sheila had sat. I scanned the living room, trying to remember where everyone had been at that moment when I asked to speak to Nora privately, Dominic approached me with a glass of wine, and Kendra and Ben headed to the other side of the living room.

Nora sat on the opposite three-seater, watching me for a reaction. "What do you think?"

I'd built up Nora's hopes only to deflate them. "I think this may have been a silly idea. People change seats for all kinds of reasons."

"Like to talk to someone different?"

"Julia said Sheila's cushion may have been uncomfortable."

"Tell Julia I don't have uncomfortable cushions."

I worked the cushion with my hands, pressing down on either side of my legs, feeling its plumpness and nodding approvingly. When I slid my hand between the cushion and the armrest, my fingers encountered a smooth, tube-shaped object. "What's this?" I gently pulled it from between the cushions. "Nora?"

"I have no idea. Let me see."

I left my couch, sat next to Nora, and handed her the tube. She peered inside one of the open ends, then slipped her finger inside and pulled. Out came a yellowed piece of paper, lined like notebook paper, with a childlike but detailed drawing of a horse and his Indian rider on it. Nora gasped.

"Is that the missing Arapaho ledger drawing?" I asked.

"It is." In a flash her countenance changed. She laid the drawing on her lap, examining every inch of it. "It's fine. I don't see any damage. What was it doing in the couch?"

I was in a bit of a pickle. I'd just finished telling Nora not to assume that Kendra was stealing from her, so how could I in good conscience tell her that Sheila and Dominic were stealing from her? If I had to guess, Dominic had stolen the drawing, placed the tube in the couch, and told his wife to safeguard it by sitting next to it. She had probably waited for the right moment to transfer the tube from the couch to her purse or coat, but her plans had been thwarted by the arrival of Gilroy and Underhill.

But all that was supposition. "Let me look into it, Nora. I have a few ideas."

"I can't call the police about this. I can't claim theft if the drawing never left my home."

She had a point. "I wonder if we might find that missing St. Vrain letter here too."

"That's a thought! I'll go over the whole house tomorrow, before Kendra and Ben arrive."

"I'll tell you something else, Nora. You were exactly right about that drawing going missing. You knew it should be there and it wasn't."

"I was right, wasn't I? I haven't fallen apart yet."

"Has anything else gone missing?"

"There's another discrepancy between the two lists. Another ledger drawing, though this one is worth less."

"Would it be easy to sell those drawings?"

"Not easy, no, but it could be done. The only complication is they're insured, so in a way they're registered to me. But a private collector would have no qualms about buying them."

What if all four of Nora's so-called friends were stealing from her? I wondered. They all had reason to, in their own minds, and they all had the means, since they were able to come and go from the documents room with ease. "Have the Wallaces or Larsons been here since Thanksgiving?"

"No, not even Kendra, and she almost lives in the documents room. She went Black Friday shopping." Nora rolled her eyes. "That's what Thanksgiving has become—shopping the Friday after, from dawn to dusk."

"Don't let Dominic or Sheila in tomorrow, either. Not

until I'm here."

"I thought as much. Sheila moved to that seat on the couch, and that's where the tube was. It's not a coincidence."

Was that why Sheila had so quickly and stridently defended Dominic against charges of theft? Because she knew he *was* stealing and it was a thorn in her conscience? "Maybe not. We'll see."

I felt a twinge of regret as I said goodbye to Nora at the door—though she didn't tell me so, I knew she wanted company—but I needed to put in another hour of writing before I quit for the night, and my energy was fading fast.

As I started down her walk, a black sedan pulled to the curb outside her house. Dominic and Sheila Larson exited the car and strode for Nora's door, Sheila cradling a pie covered in plastic wrap. Dominic's imitation of a smile, ready to greet Nora in faux innocence, hardened to a grimace when he saw me. "What are you doing here?"

"Dominic, stop it," Sheila said.

I did an about-face for Nora's door and knocked. "I was just getting some fresh air."

When Nora opened the door, I stepped back into her house, ignoring her perplexed expression. "Actually, Nora invited me to stay the night and have a look at her documents. For some research I'm doing."

"Really?" Dominic said.

After a moment's pause, Nora caught on. "Yes, I think Rachel's mysteries could do with a touch of Colorado history, and since it's late, why make her drive home? What are you two doing here this time of night?"

"I brought you a pie," Sheila said.

"A pie," Nora repeated. "At this hour?"

I gave Nora a warning look, removed my coat, and

took a few steps into the living room before turning back around. *I'm not leaving, Dominic and Sheila. I'll be here all night. So forget about retrieving your drawing.*

"Well, you'd best come in, then," Nora said, taking the pie from Sheila.

Dominic quickly retreated. "We can't stay. Sorry for disturbing you." Before he left, he pulled himself to his full height, smiled at me, and in a buttery voice said, "See you later this week, Rachel."

# CHAPTER 11

I spent an uncomfortable night in Nora's overheated house, lying on top of an old bedspread on a spare bed, wondering at first if the Larsons would try to return. But when I remembered my Forester was parked outside, serving as a deterrent, it wasn't long before I fell asleep. Before seven the next morning, I was on my way home, hungry for toast and coffee in my own kitchen. And before I'd finished half my breakfast, Julia was at my door.

I made Julia a cup of coffee and told her about Nora's missing drawing, her found drawing, the Larsons' surprise pie visit, and my sleepover. True to form, she wanted to leave that instant and give the Larsons what-for on Nora's behalf. Barring that, she wanted to tell Chief Gilroy what Dominic and his wife were up to.

"He's not going to charge them with theft if the drawing was still in Nora's house," I pointed out. "Though we should tell him about the discrepancies in those printouts and how I found the tube in the couch."

"Do you think the Larsons stole the miniature?"

"I don't know," I said, pouring myself a second cup of hazelnut coffee. "Right now I'm more interested in who took it to Anne's room after it was stolen. I'm driving out to Aspen Glen. Feel like going with me before we head to

Holly's Sweets?"

"You bet. I'm ready."

"Just let me finish my coffee," I said, dropping to a seat at my kitchen table. "I need my caffeine."

"Bad night?"

"How do people sleep in an eighty-degree house?"

"Was it that hot?"

"Probably not, but it felt like it."

"I've told Nora she should get her blood checked. It's not normal to like it so hot. She needs to eat more, too. She's skin and bones."

I opened my mouth to speak but clamped it shut. Conversation between the two of us had become effortless in the six months I'd been Julia's neighbor, and I was so used to discussing nearly everything with her that I'd almost let slip Nora's Alzheimer's diagnosis. In time, Julia would know, and it wasn't my place to tell her. "I'm ready," I said, carrying my cup to the sink. "Let me grab my keys."

Fifteen minutes later we were at Aspen Glen, standing at the front desk and trying to ply a new receptionist for information without the tongue-loosening benefit of Holly's donuts. A couple of fruitless minutes later, I decided to take a new tack and ask to see Donna and Betty.

"Go on in," the receptionist said. "I think they're by the fireplace. They like their coffee out there."

I spotted them in the same place they'd been on Friday, sitting near Frank. Frank was reading his morning paper, Betty was sipping from a Blue Willow cup, and Donna was wrapped in a different but equally thick sweater.

"Hello there," Betty said. "I remember you. And you've brought a friend."

Frank looked up from his paper and glanced at my

hands, probably looking for a pink box, I thought.

"This is my friend Julia," I said. "Julia, this is Frank, Betty, and Donna."

"Frank is looking for donuts," Donna said with an impish smile.

"I'm doing no such thing," he said, holding his paper up and snapping it with his wrists.

"I can bring some on Sunday, if you'd like," I said, sitting next to Frank and motioning for Julia to join me. "But today I wanted to ask you all a few questions about Anne."

"Is Chief Gilroy coming?" Betty asked.

"He's not here with me, but he may come on his own."

"Are you still trying to figure out what happened to her?" Donna asked.

"I am."

"Then ask me anything."

"Good for you," Julia said. "Anne deserves our help."

"Did you know her too?" Frank said.

"Not as well as all of you, but yes. I used to meet her at Nora's."

Mention of Nora, the angel who had enabled Anne to live at Aspen Glen, opened the floodgates. Julia was a friend and ally.

Betty leaned toward her and whispered, "She was pushed down the stairs."

"I know," Julia said. "We've been telling everyone since it happened. It was no accident."

"People think anyone over fifty is liable to fall down the stairs at any moment," Betty said. "Ridiculous."

"Tell me about it," Julia said, bristling with indignation.

Realizing we were about to go down a rabbit hole, I

interrupted. "Did any of you notice if someone from outside Aspen Glen visited on Thanksgiving evening?" I asked.

"We usually have visitors on holidays," Frank said. "Donna? Betty?"

"There were three women from our church, but I think they were here while it was still light out," Betty said.

"Your family, Frank," Donna said.

"I don't think that's what the young lady is asking," Frank said.

"There was a man who brought a vase of flowers," Donna said.

"That was Evelyn's son," Frank said.

"And that young woman with the leftovers," Donna said.

My head jerked. "What young woman? What did she look like?"

"I remember her," Frank answered. "Average height, pretty, blonde."

"She came late in the day, said she didn't want them to spoil and hoped we'd enjoy a late-night snack," Betty said. "How I used to love eating turkey sandwiches on Thanksgiving night. It was a treat to do it again."

"Where was she?" I asked, waving my hands in the air. "I mean, in the building. Did you see where she went?"

Betty lifted her head and stared at the ceiling. "In the lobby, of course. But she also was on the first floor. Not the second, I think. She wasn't here long enough."

"Where on the first floor?" I asked.

"She went down the hall." Betty pointed down the corridor we had walked on Friday. Anne's corridor.

"Did anyone go with her?"

"There was no reason to," Donna said.

I nodded and turned to Julia. "That's all we need."

"Why would Paige—" Julia began.

"I'll try to bring donuts on Sunday," I said, lightening my tone as I interrupted her. Mentioning Paige meant, eventually, mentioning her death, and there was no way I was going to do that. "Any requests?"

"Chocolate," Frank said.

"I like the glazed," Betty said.

"Any jelly donut," Donna said.

"Jelly's my favorite," I said.

"Did we help you solve Anne's murder?" Betty asked.

"You answered a very important question," I replied. "A crucial one."

"If Chief Gilroy has any questions, tell him we're happy to be of help," Donna said. "Anytime. He doesn't have to call first. He can stop by."

Betty shook her head. "No call necessary."

"I'll let him know," I said, getting to my feet. Hiding a grin, or trying to, I made my way to the door, Julia puffing to keep up with me.

"What's all that about Chief Gilroy?" Julia said once we'd settled into the Forester.

"They like him. A lot." I backed out of the parking space and drove east for Holly's Sweets.

"I like him too, but I don't act like that. Do I?"

"No, nothing so obvious," I said.

"Good." Julia paused a beat and then twisted my way in her seat. "What do you mean?"

"Nothing, Julia. Let's focus on what you're going to say to Sheila Larson, now that you know about that Arapaho drawing hidden in Nora's couch."

"Good idea." Julia straightened and leaned back on the

headrest. "That drawing explains why Sheila changed seats."

"Probably, but I'm not totally convinced."

"I'll find out. Poor Nora. She trusted them."

"I need to talk to Kendra and find out why Nora's list of items doesn't match hers."

"Kendra and Ben are stealing from Nora too."

"Maybe."

I parked across the street from the bakery, checked my car clock, and turned off my engine. "Ten minutes to nine. I hope she hasn't been here already."

"We should have walkie-talkies," Julia said.

"Better yet, earbuds like secret service agents wear."

"Wish me luck."

"Where are you going to wait?"

"Outside the bakery door. The sun's warm."

"Won't that look a little suspicious?"

Julia waved me off. "I'm short and old. Who's going to notice?"

I was taken aback by her words. It sounded as though she were relinquishing any future claim on happiness. Before she exited the car, I put a hand on her arm. "Holly and I would notice. I don't know what we'd do without you."

She looked back at me, her eyes glazed with tears. "I feel the same way about the two of you."

"Julia, what's going on? You're not leaving this car until you tell me."

She sat on the edge of her seat, her feet dangling over the pavement. "It's Nora. She has Alzheimer's."

It didn't cross my mind to feign surprise. I couldn't lie to my friend. "I found out last night."

"She told you?"

"I guessed and she confirmed."

"What is she going to do, Rachel?"

"Right now she's in the early stages. She remembered those drawings were in her documents room once—that takes a good memory."

"She's all alone."

"She's not alone. She has friends. And she *won't be* alone."

"It's ironic. She took care of Anne for years." With a sudden intake of breath, Julia slid down from the seat. "That's Sheila! She just went in the bakery."

I rolled down my window, calling to her as she made her way around the front of my car. "Be careful."

Julia left the bakery two minutes later, Sheila on her heels, snapping like an angry dog. I got out and darted across the street.

"And don't you ever talk to me again," Sheila was saying.

"I didn't mean to offend you," Julia said, her brow creased in innocence and confusion—an expression she excelled at.

"What's going on?" I said.

"*You.*" Her anger mounting, Sheila's eyes became slits and she jutted out her chin. "I should have known. You put her up to this."

"I can put my own self up, thank you very much," Julia said.

I counted to three before I spoke. I was on the verge of losing my temper, watching Sheila berate Julia. The nerve. She was the one stealing. "I'd really like it if no one went to jail over this. Things can be put right before it's too late."

Sheila recoiled. "Jail?" And just like that, she was meek again.

"Do you think you can steal valuable artifacts and people are going to shrug and walk away?"

An expression of utter bewilderment came over her face. "I haven't done anything. I haven't stolen anything from anybody."

"The ledger drawing, Sheila," I said.

"What drawing?" she asked.

"The one you tried to steal at Nora's," Julia said.

"No. No, I don't know . . ."

Sheila seemed so baffled by my assertion that I was beginning to believe her. But a moment later, another look crossed her face: recognition.

"I need to go," she said.

"Dominic asked you to change seats at Thanksgiving, didn't he?" I said.

"Why do you two keep asking me about seats?"

"Because the drawing was hidden in a tube stuck between your cushion and the armrest," I said. "When you sat there, you ensured that no one would find it."

"No, that's not possible."

"You have to talk to your husband," I said. "Or this is going to end very badly."

Sheila's face was white and drained, and she kept shaking her head as if she were answering no to questions only she could hear. When she twisted her red hair in her fingers, I saw the same Sheila I'd seen at Nora's. A worried child.

"Sheila, you had a feeling Dominic was up to something," I said.

"No, I didn't," she said. "And he's not up to anything wrong. He's a good man, Rachel. Don't you dare say another word. I'm done listening to you." With that, she stormed down the sidewalk and darted into the street, inches ahead of a screeching car.

# CHAPTER 12

After picking up some scones at the bakery and filling Holly in on the latest, Julia and I hurried to Nora's house. I'd offered to drive Julia home, but she'd insisted on staying with Nora while "those ungrateful thieves," Kendra and Ben, were in her house.

We made it to Nora's a little before ten, just ahead of the Wallaces, who were forced to park behind us on Nora's driveway. The scones were my excuse for showing up and staying awhile. I figured Nora, Julia, and I would have a nice midmorning break—in the documents room.

"Rachel, Julia, how lovely," Nora said, meeting us at the door.

"I've got scones fresh from Holly's Sweets," I said, handing her the box and draping my coat over the back of the first armchair in the living room.

"Kendra, Ben," Nora said, "you remember Rachel and Julia from Thanksgiving."

"Actually, we met Rachel again at the Historical Society," Kendra said. "She stopped by to let us know the miniature had been found."

"And take a tour of the soon-to-be museum," Ben said. He was in a suit and red tie again. His uniform for working in Nora's house, I supposed.

"Drop your coats, everyone," Nora said. "We're going to have coffee and scones."

"Um, well . . ." Ben motioned at the stairs. "Kendra and I need to get to work. We only have a couple hours, so . . ."

"Then let's have our scones in the documents room," I said. "Nora?"

Kendra was horrified. "Scones are one thing, but coffee? With all those precious papers?"

"We won't spill, we're not children," Nora said. "You take the scones, Rachel. Julia and I will start the coffee."

Nora pushed the box into my hands, and with a simple, authoritative nod of her head, she both ended the discussion and commanded me and the Wallaces to take ourselves to the documents room.

"What's gotten into her?" Ben said, trudging up the stairs.

Kendra flipped the light switch and flung open the drapes. I did my best to stand lookout over the contents of the documents room while Julia and Nora were downstairs, though I think Kendra found my silence and roving eyes unnerving. But I was afraid she would fold a document and stuff it in her jeans pocket, or that Ben would tuck a St. Vrain letter in his shoes, if I lost concentration for one moment. I was relieved when I heard Nora and Julia on the stairs. This job needed three pairs of eyes.

When Kendra gazed into the glass front of a cabinet door, her face fell. She yanked it open and began to frantically search the shelves. "Where is it? Where's the miniature?"

"Here we are," Nora said, placing a tray of cups on the little table by the door. Julia set a coffeepot—Wedgwood

Blue Willow, I noticed—on the tray. "The miniature is in a safe place outside the documents room. Serve yourselves." She sat with a sigh on the office chair. "You haven't eaten those scones yet, have you?"

"We haven't touched them." I held the open box before her, like a waiter presenting a restaurant's dessert tray. "Blueberry, currant, and chocolate."

Delighted, Nora clasped her hands together, and once again I was struck by how she found pleasure in the simplest things. But she worked at it, I thought. It didn't come naturally to her. She *wanted* to savor life.

"Goodness," Kendra sighed. "I was worried."

"No need," Nora said.

"I'll take chocolate," Julia said, pouring herself a cup of coffee.

A sidelong glance passed between Kendra and Ben. Coffee and scones amid the historical documents? Such barbarians. I might have laughed if I hadn't been working so hard at trying to find a way to broach the subject of the mismatched printouts. Kendra couldn't have known that Nora had her own printout—an old one, as it turned out. If she had, she never would have brazenly revised her own to hide the thefts of at least three items.

I poured myself some coffee, remarking on Nora's cups. "They have Wedgwood Blue Willow at Aspen Glen. Beautiful cups and saucers, with a crisply printed pattern, just like these."

"Those are mine," Nora said. "I had twenty place settings. Who on earth needs all that?"

"But you have dinner parties," Kendra said.

"Did we lack for china at Thanksgiving?" Nora answered. "Not that we ever got to use it."

"Are there any other chairs?" Julia asked, glancing about the room.

"I'll get some," Ben said, making an eager exit. He seemed anxious in the presence of so many intruders in his private domain. He thought of Nora as an intruder too, I was sure.

*Now is as good a time as any*, I thought. "Kendra, how do you keep track of everything in this room?"

"I'm a librarian at heart," she said, folding her arms and leaning against a glass-doored cabinet. "I love bringing order to collections."

"You'd have to, wouldn't you?" I said with a grin. "But how do you do it? What's your process?"

"I couldn't do it without a computer. Once I've assessed an item, it goes into my database, and I physically place the item on its proper shelf or in its proper box or file. I mix things up once in a while, but generally, I'm moving from left to right in the room. I've got a long way to go. I haven't started on the shelves in the middle of the room or the cabinets behind you."

Giving the room a closer inspection, I saw there was a neatness and order to one of the bookcases on the far wall.

Ben returned carrying a wooden chair in each hand. "Well, I'm having a cup of coffee," he said, giving one chair to Julia and the other to me.

"The documents," Kendra protested.

"I know how to drink without spilling," he said.

"So Kendra," I said, "why was the miniature in a cabinet you hadn't cataloged yet? Just out of curiosity."

She lifted her shoulders. "I found a bare and safe spot behind glass."

"Not that safe, as it turned out," Nora said, breaking off

a bit of scone and popping it into her mouth.

"No, but then it didn't go back inside the cabinet," Kendra said. Her words were a direct challenge to Nora, who had left the miniature on the desk rather than putting it back in the cabinet.

Ben stepped in. "It wouldn't have made any difference. We all saw Anne take it, and she could have easily taken it from the cabinet. None of us said a word. We let her do it."

"Because we'd been asked to let her do it," Kendra said, again questioning Nora's judgment. "It wasn't the first thing she took from this room."

Nora laid what was left of her scone on the desk and brushed her hands over it, sending crumbs everywhere. "Anne thought she was helping me, as you both know. She always gave me back what she took."

"She didn't this time," Kendra said.

"She couldn't," I said. "She wasn't the one who took it out of the house."

"I think we've established that," Ben said. "You never did say how it ended up in Anne's room at Aspen Glen."

"That's right," Nora said, swiveling my way in her chair. "Do you know?"

There was no harm in telling them. The miniature was back home and Paige was out of their grasps. Anyway, I wanted to see their reactions. "Paige took it out of the house in a container of mashed potatoes. Then later on Thanksgiving, she took it to Aspen Glen."

Kendra and Ben looked as though they'd been slapped.

"Paige took it?" Nora said. "Are you sure?"

"I'm afraid so."

"Paige?" Nora repeated. "In mashed potatoes?"

"She put that gem in mashed potatoes?" Kendra said.

"She wrapped it first," I said. I bit my tongue to keep from smiling. Suddenly the thought of that miniature, everyone's obsession, sitting in a mound of mashed potatoes was funny.

"What was Paige thinking?" Kendra said.

"Calm down, it's safe now," Ben said.

Kendra jabbed a thumb in her husband's direction. "To Ben, that miniature is a curiosity. To me, it's irreplaceable."

"I believe historical facts are more important, that's all," Ben said. "I can live without this fascination with originals. Though I have to say, holding something St. Vrain once owned is thrilling."

It was time to steer the conversation back to record keeping in the documents room. "How do you decide if a record or artifact is authentic, Kendra?"

"It's a cinch in this room. Almost everything in it has an excellent provenance. Did you know that St. Vrain met Nora's great-great-grandfather? That's documented. And her great-grandfather, grandfather, and so on were avid collectors who kept records. I'm able to focus on cataloging rather than exploring authenticity."

I shifted focus to Ben. "That must make writing your dissertation easier. You have a gold mine of authentic documents at your fingertips."

"Nora's been kind enough to let me do my research here," Ben said. "There's no better place to be, and that includes the University of Colorado. I've cut my research time in half because most of what I need is in this room." He spread out his arms.

"Was the miniature a help in any way?"

"It was. No other historian has had access to it, and it proves what's only been suggested before—that St. Vrain and the artist, Henry Dobbs, met in Washington, D.C. the year it was painted. It alters the St. Vrain time line. It's not often that a modern-day historian can change what's been assumed about a person or event for decades or centuries. And naturally, this all begs the question. How did St. Vrain and Dobbs meet? What was their relationship?"

Kendra's attention had started to wander as soon as I'd stopped talking to her and started talking to Ben, and now she was openly yawning and making a show of checking her wristwatch, as if to say, *My work is much more important than yours*. They weren't on edge, as Ben had said at the Historical Society. They were at odds.

"When is your dissertation due?" I asked.

"About six weeks. It's crunch time."

"Anywaaay," Kendra said, elongating the word, "speaking of crunch time, I should get to work."

Kendra moved for the desk, but Nora didn't budge.

"We have a problem," Nora said.

"What's that?" Kendra said.

"I want answers."

Nora had lost patience. Diplomacy was about to go out the window.

"I think what Nora is referring to is a discrepancy she found," I said.

Nora opened a book on the desk, removed the folded printouts from its pages, and smoothed them open. "Come here, Kendra."

Kendra peered at the lists, then reached out and angled them her way. "Printouts from my cataloging."

"I kept a copy of my own for safekeeping," Nora said. "I came in here after hours and ran it out on the printer. What you're looking at are my copy and your copy."

Kendra drew back her hand, squinting in confusion. "You've lost me."

Nora pointed. "Let's start with item 22. It was an Arapaho ledger drawing with an estimated worth of over seven hundred dollars. It's on my list but doesn't appear on yours."

"Why not?" Ben said.

Kendra glared at him over her shoulder. "She's accusing me of stealing it, Ben."

"I'm not accusing, I'm asking," Nora said.

"I remember that drawing," Kendra said, angrily crossing her arms. "An Arapaho warrior and his horse. You have a number of other drawings from the same ledger book."

"I know. Another ledger drawing is also missing."

"Is that what you're all doing here?" Ben asked. "Scones and coffee?"

Kendra pressed a button on the computer, causing it to spring to life. "Get up," she ordered Nora. "Let me look." She popped open a file, scrolled her way down, and studied the screen. "It's not here. It should be here. I typed it into this file and I put the drawing in that box." She flung a hand in the direction of the orderly bookcase across the room.

"It's not there," Nora said.

"I can't believe you'd suggest that I—"

"Hang on, let's not all fly off the handle," Ben said, desperation in his voice. He needed access to Nora's documents for his dissertation and was terrified of losing it.

"Ben's right," I said. "All we know is that the drawings were taken. We don't know who took them, and right now, only one of them is still missing."

Kendra turned on me. "Did you accuse me behind my

back?"

"Like you accused Dominic behind his?" I retorted. "No, I didn't."

"On the contrary, Rachel has told me to remain neutral," Nora said.

Julia cleared her throat—loudly. "I heard the doorbell."

"I'll get it," I said, charging out the door before the others could act. If I didn't get away from Kendra, I'd say something I'd regret.

I hurried downstairs, marched for the door, and was astonished to find Chief Gilroy on the front step, about to hit the doorbell again.

"Rachel?"

"Chief," I said. "James. I mean . . . I don't know what to call you."

"What are you doing here?"

"Visiting. With scones." I almost smacked my own forehead. "Come in, I'll get Nora."

"I'm right here," Nora said, cutting a path across the living room. "Chief Gilroy, what can I do for you?"

Gilroy dug into his coat pocket and presented Nora with a plastic bag, and what appeared to be a gold locket inside it. "I wonder if you could identify this."

"My word." Nora turned it over in her hands. "It belonged to my grandmother."

# CHAPTER 13

Julia and I decided to head to Wyatt's Bistro to talk about the latest turn of events: Gilroy's discovery of Nora's locket in Anne Rightler's old room at Aspen Glen. He'd found it in a second search of the room, an hour before a new resident moved in. I could tell its sudden appearance bothered him. He wouldn't have missed that locket in the first search. So how did it magically manifest itself in Anne's room? And why?

I told Gilroy about Paige bringing her leftovers to Aspen Glen on Thanksgiving night and sneaking the miniature into Anne's room, and I suggested that he talk to the residents, telling him they were an observant bunch, all things considered. And then he cautioned me again about getting involved, though for once he didn't use the word "meddle."

Kendra had left a minute after Gilroy had shown up, pouting her way out the door, an apologetic Ben right behind her. Julia had waited until she could hear them both in the living room before relinquishing her guard over the documents room. When we left, Nora promised us she wouldn't allow the Wallaces or Larsons inside her house until Anne and Paige's killer had been found, and I believed her. She was a trusting woman at heart, and her friends' betrayals hurt her deeply.

I found a vacant parking spot half a block from Wyatt's, shut off the car, and turned to Julia. "I'm beginning to wonder if everyone who was in Nora's house on Thanksgiving wasn't stealing from her. Anne wasn't doing it maliciously, but the other four? It's looking like there were two husband-and-wife teams looting her house. Not to be nosy, but is Nora wealthy?"

"She's well off, but I wouldn't say wealthy. She has enough to invest through Dominic. But she's going to need care in the years ahead, and that's going to take a lot of money. I've told her to sell that miniature and put the money in the bank. She needs it more than any old museum does."

"I hope she does that."

Julia jammed her fingers into her short, gray hair, plumping it up. "Have you looked closely at that thing? It's ugly. You couldn't pay me to put in my house."

"True. The watercolors in Wyatt's are better. But it's a piece of history."

"If you ask me, that Dobbs fellow was running a scam. He was no artist. I'm going to tell Nora again—sell that thing and keep the money."

"After this morning, and Dominic and Sheila paying a surprise visit last night, I think Nora might do it. She might cut them *all* off. Let's go inside. I didn't get one of those scones, and I'm starving."

We found a somewhat private corner table, ordered lunch, and got down to the business of the locket.

"Nora said that locket was in her bedroom," I pointed out. "That means someone is poking around Nora's house and stealing from other rooms."

"Do you think Paige took more than the miniature?"

"It's hard to believe that was the first thing she stole from Nora's house, but Paige didn't have the connections the Wallaces and Larsons have, so how would she sell what she took?"

"Do you think Paige murdered Anne to get the miniature?"

Our waiter interrupted, bringing us our sandwiches, which gave me time to consider Julia's question. I wanted to say no, but truthfully, it was possible. At Thanksgiving, Paige had grumbled about money—how the Wallaces and Larsons argued over it when they had so much, how she'd have to pay for the wine glass she broke—and money was a classic motive for murder. After the waiter left, I said, "If Paige didn't kill Anne, how did she get the miniature? That's the problem."

"Maybe Anne set it down in the kitchen or restroom?"

I shook my head. "You saw how she guarded it."

"One of the Wallaces or Larsons picked her pocket when she wasn't looking?"

"Anne patted the miniature several times. She kept checking. Just the weight of it in her cardigan—she would have noticed if it disappeared."

As I ate my BLT and watched the other diners, I tried to come up with scenarios that didn't involve Paige as a murderer. Kendra, Ben, Dominic, and Sheila were more likely to be killers in my book, but they'd never had possession of the miniature.

Or had they? I knew Anne had the painting before she died, and that Paige had hidden it in a container of leftovers in order to take it from the house, but the journey between those two points was a mystery. The simplest solution was that Paige took it from Anne and then pushed her down the stairs to cover the theft. But that didn't make sense to me.

"If Paige killed Anne," I said, "why was Paige killed?"

"Revenge?" Julia said, talking through her egg salad.

"For taking the miniature?"

"It seems like an overreaction when the killer could have just taken the monstrosity back."

"But he or she couldn't. By Thanksgiving night, it was in Anne's room."

"Then we're back to revenge."

"And new scenarios."

"Look who just walked in." Julia shifted in her seat, trying to make herself invisible. "I think he sees us."

"Too late," I said under my breath. In a few quick strides of his long legs, Dominic Larson was at our table.

"What a surprise," he said, towering over Julia. This was a man accustomed to using his height to intimidate.

"Please join us," I said.

From the corner of my eye I saw Julia jerk her head toward me. But it was either ask Dominic to sit, and so bring him down to our level, or allow him to loom over us like the Sears Tower.

"My pleasure," he said. He dragged out a chair and sank down into it. "So what are we talking about? Wait, let me guess. Killers and thieves, cops and robbers. Am I right?" Delighted by his own witty banter, he rubbed his hands together.

"I thought you cared about Paige," I said. "You seemed genuinely upset when you found out she'd been murdered."

Dominic stared at me as though I'd committed a great social faux pas. "I liked Paige, and yes, I was upset. What's with you?"

"You're joking about killers," I said.

"All right, just thieves, then. We'll forget the killers. Happy? It's obvious Paige *was* a thief, though. But so was Anne Rightler."

"How well did you know Anne?"

"Not well. I knew she stole things from Nora. Every time she was at her house. Nora let her do it. She patted her on the head, never called the police. It drove me crazy. I insured those things, and they were at risk."

"I thought you liked Anne too."

"I got a kick out of her. She was a nice old woman, but she shouldn't have taken that miniature. We were all in the documents room, talking about how precious it was, remember? Anne even asked if it was precious, and Kendra said yes. So instead of taking something insignificant, she took *that*. What if it had been damaged?"

"Luckily for all of you, it wasn't in her pocket when she was pushed down the stairs."

"I didn't say Anne's death—look, I don't believe she was pushed down the stairs. Have the police said that?"

"The Thanksgiving holiday delayed the medical examiner's report. We'll know the official cause of death soon."

"Only half of it." Dominic scanned the table. "Water glass?"

"Take mine," I said, sliding it his way. "What do you mean half?"

"We'll know how she died but not who killed her." He fished his wallet out of an inside coat pocket, picked through the slots, and extracted a foil packet. "Ibuprofen," he said. "I wrenched my back."

"Sorry to hear that. How did it happen?"

"Moving boxes in the basement." He tore open the

pack and took two pills, downing half his water.

"So who do *you* think killed Paige and Anne?"

"Ben, Kendra, or Nora, because it wasn't me and it wasn't Sheila."

Julia, who up until now had remained silent, gasped and shook a finger at him. "You should be ashamed. You make your living from Nora's money and you accuse her of murder? That tells me it was *you*, Dominic Larson. Only a bad man would shift blame to a decent woman."

"I'm only looking at things logically, Julia."

"Logically," I said, "what was Nora's reason for killing Anne?"

"She stole the one thing from that documents room that really mattered to Nora. Somehow Paige did the same thing. I heard she's the one who got the miniature out of Nora's house."

I ignored his unspoken question: How did she do it? I sensed that he already knew. "It didn't matter to Nora half as much as it mattered to Kendra."

"Then Kendra did it." He slipped his wallet into his coat and stood.

"Logically, what was her reason?" I asked, gazing upward.

"Ask Kendra. I lost track of how many times she said she could murder 'that old lady' for touching her precious artifacts. The same would apply to Paige."

"And Ben?" I said, asking before he could walk away. "Logically?"

"Anne risked damaging the artifact that would change the St. Vrain time line," he said, wiggling his fingers in mock excitement. "The vaunted St. Vrain time line. He couldn't take a chance it would happen again, and he was angry with

Paige because she could have lost the miniature forever."

"Ben didn't care if he didn't have the original," I countered.

"His dissertation director would," Dominic said. "He promised he was basing his dissertation in part on a newly found artifact."

He left without another word, his giant legs taking him to the front door, where Sheila was waiting for him. How long had she been standing there? I wondered. They seated themselves at a two-seat table near the door.

"I've noticed that Dominic never helps Sheila with her coat or stands for her," I said.

"Murderers aren't polite," Julia said, returning to her sandwich. "He put me off my food."

"There's something funny about him."

"Accusing Nora."

"I'm not saying he's the killer."

"I'll say it."

"We should meet again tonight. The gang."

"I'm ready."

"I don't like the feeling I'm getting, Julia. I think Nora's in danger."

Julia dropped her sandwich to her plate. "From Dominic?"

"If I knew that, I'd tell Gilroy. I need more information."

"Then you get it. I'll lose my friend soon enough, but not this way. Not this way."

# CHAPTER 14

"I need to do some research of my own," I said, heading west on Main Street.

"The library?" Julia asked.

"My computer."

My latest encounters with Dominic and the Wallaces had given me an idea—a new avenue of approach. What did I know about this St. Vrain? Nothing, really. I saw his name from time to time. A Colorado river, school district, state park, valley, and even soccer club bore his name. It was time to do some digging.

When I turned the corner onto Finch Hill Road, I saw a police SUV, its lights flashing red and blue, sitting in front of my house—and Holly outside my front gate, leaning in, waiting. She heard my car, spun back, and waved me down.

I lurched to a stop behind the SUV and hopped out.

"You're all right!" Holly cried, rushing over to me. I stared, bewildered, and she hugged me. "As long as you're all right."

"What's happening on my street?" Julia said.

Holly laughed and brushed back a tear. "Oh, Julia, you always take things personally. How I love you."

Julia's hands went to her hips. "Holly Kavanagh, what's going on?"

"Yes, what?" I said. "Is that Gilroy in my house?" I started for my gate but she pulled me back.

"He just got here. He hasn't had time to search it yet."

"Search it? Why?"

"Now, be calm. I took the afternoon off from the bakery, and I stopped by with a cream puff, and—"

"Oh, for goodness' sake," Julia said, rolling her eyes.

"And I noticed your front door was open," Holly went on. "I walked into the living room and looked through to the kitchen, and I saw someone had opened your back door."

I couldn't believe my ears. Someone had invaded my home.

"I ran out and called Gilroy. I'm sorry."

"What are you sorry for?" I said.

"Running and maybe leaving you inside."

"You had to run. *Of course* you run. Don't be silly. Anyone could be in there." Now it was my turn to hug Holly. "What are you going to do, fight them with a pastry box?"

"I dropped it in the living room."

"Well, let us pray the cream puff made it through the experience," Julia said.

I saw Gilroy trotting down my porch steps and hurried to meet him in my front garden.

"There's no one in there," he said, holding up his hands, trying to reassure me. "It's fine."

"It's *not* fine," I said. Inside, I was shaking.

"Your back door was broken into, your front door is okay, and I don't see any damage inside, but I'd like you to walk me through it."

I nodded and numbly followed him into my house while Julia and Holly waited on the porch.

"Your front door still locks," Gilroy said, closing it

behind him. "It's your back door I'm concerned about. It looks like they used a crowbar to pry the molding and get around the deadbolt."

"They?"

"A figure of speech. Are you all right?"

I nodded again. "It's a cheap door and an even cheaper lock."

"Do you see anything wrong in the living room?"

"No. Did you check upstairs too?"

"Everywhere. Including the closets, the cabinets, and under your bed."

"Just like you'd search for monsters," I mumbled.

We went over my house room by room, but to my surprise, nothing was missing and nothing other than my back door was damaged. Whoever broke in hadn't even touched my computer. Someone was trying to scare me by showing me they could enter my house at any time, and they were doing a good job of it. Gilroy took a pen and notebook from inside his coat and we sat at my kitchen table.

"Officer Underhill will be here any moment now to dust for prints, but I have to tell you, I'm not optimistic," he said.

"I'm sure they used gloves."

"They might not be in the system."

"That depends. Do the Wallaces or Larsons have police records?"

I heard the front door creak open and Officer Underhill call for Gilroy. "Ready to dust," he said, striding eagerly into the kitchen carrying a black plastic case—his fingerprint kit. He was in his glory.

"Start with the front and back doors," Gilroy said. "Rachel, we'll need your prints for elimination. Tomorrow at the station? Mrs. Foster's and Mrs. Kavanagh's too, if they would."

"Tomorrow's Sunday," I said.

"Is it? I've lost track of time. Make it Monday, then."

I could hear Underhill humming a cheery tune as he set to work on the front door. "You need to hire another officer."

"I did. He starts in one week."

"When did that happen?"

"I just got the go-ahead from the mayor and Board of Trustees."

So that's why Underhill was humming. "Maybe you and Underhill can get some sleep now."

"What time did you leave your house this morning?" Gilroy asked.

"About a quarter to eight. This is the first time I've been back all day." I lowered my chin into my hand. "Ben and Kendra Wallace left Nora's house before I did," I said. "You saw them. They couldn't leave fast enough."

"Do you think they did this?"

"I think they were stealing from Nora. Though Kendra looked genuinely shocked that her database had been changed, and she wasn't the only one who had access to it."

"You're going to have to back up there."

For the next few minutes I went over the discrepancies Nora had shown me in the two printouts, and I told him about the recovered ledger drawing. A little frown furrowed his brow now and then, but Gilroy listened to me and never once asked me what on earth I was up to now—though I could tell those words were on the tip of his tongue.

"Nora thinks Kendra edited the catalog file so there would be no record of the drawing and she could sell it to finance her museum," I said. "If it wasn't Kendra, it was Ben or one of the others. Someone changed that file so they could steal artifacts. It's pretty easy pickings. I don't think Nora knows half of what's in her documents room, and those four have—or had—free run of the house."

"Found some good prints," Underhill said, strolling toward my back door. "But they're probably yours, Rachel."

"I wonder why Paige put the miniature in Anne's room," I said absentmindedly.

"A guilty conscience," Underhill said, dipping his brush into the lid of a fingerprint powder jar. "But she couldn't take it back to Nora Barberton's house or she'd be caught. She knew she was taking leftovers to Aspen Glen, and voilà."

*That's not a bad theory*, I thought. Underhill surprised me.

"Or she wanted to make it look like Anne had taken it," he added.

"Mrs. Rightler was dead before the miniature was found," Gilroy reminded him.

Underhill began to spin his brush over and around the doorknob, depositing his black powder. "Oh, yeah, that's right. The days and hours are running into each other. But not for long, eh, Chief?" He looked back at Gilroy, a huge smile on his face, and Gilroy smiled back.

"Can we come in?" Julia called, edging her way from the living room into the kitchen. "We won't touch anything."

"Sure," Gilroy said, rising from the table and offering Julia his seat.

Holly walked in behind Julia, the pink pastry box in her hand. "It landed face up," she said.

"Thank heaven for that," Julia said. "I don't know how I would have slept, thinking the box had overturned."

Holly set the box gently, slowly in the middle of the table, as though it held a delicate treasure, and then shot Julia an exaggerated scowl.

"There won't be any useful fingerprints," I said.

"Let's not give up just yet," Underhill said. As he snapped photos of the gray-powder prints around my doorknob, he started whistling.

"Rachel, I think you should stay elsewhere tonight," Gilroy said. "Until you can get a locksmith to fix that door and install a better deadbolt."

"I have an idea," Holly said. "Pizza here this evening, the three of us, and then you sleep at my house tonight."

"You get up at four o'clock in the morning," Julia said. "Rachel can stay at my house."

"Sounds like you have two good options," Gilroy said, looking pleased. I realized then that he'd allowed Julia and Holly into the house so they would hear his warning to me and take action.

The gravity of the break-in was beginning to sink in. Replacing a door and staying with Julia or Holly was easy, but my sense of security wouldn't return until the culprit was caught.

"Why are you looking so glum?" Holly asked me. "They didn't steal anything, you're safe, and you'll fix the door tomorrow."

"Someone was in my house, probably touching my things. And I'd like to sleep in my own bed tonight."

"Don't," Gilroy said.

"What if they come back and steal something?"

"Do you want to be here if they do?"

"Good point."

"I don't think they will, Rachel," he said, "but I don't

want you to risk your safety on my hunch. I'm asking you to stay with one of your friends."

Julia, who I feared was on the verge of saying *aww*, rose from the table. "You wanted to go shopping, Rachel?"

*I did?* "Okay. Sure."

"Let me take care of a few things next door and I'll be back," Julia said before making a quick exit.

"Me too," Holly said. "I'll be right back—wait for me."

Underhill had finished his task at the back door and was packing up his fingerprint kit. "Do you have a two-by-four or something like it?" he asked. "I could nail it across the door to keep it from opening when the wind blows or something."

"Excellent idea," Gilroy said.

"I've got a few pieces of wood in my garage that should do the job. I'll get one."

"You stay there," Underhill said. "Garage door key?" he asked, taking my key ring from a hook by the door.

"The one with the green key cover," I replied. "Thank you, Officer."

The sound of Underhill rolling back my garage door seemed loud in the sudden silence of the kitchen. Gilroy fastened his blue eyes on me. Why had I ever thought they were cold? They were pale, but pale as a mountain lake. The loveliest eyes I'd ever seen.

"Promise me you're not going to stay here alone," he said.

"I promise."

"If you stayed here, I'd worry all night."

"I'll stay with Julia or Holly."

"Good."

I let loose a long sigh and slumped back in my chair. "You know, after eighty-seven years of life, Anne Rightler deserved better than to die the way she did. And Nora . . . I can't say why, but she needs my help." I had changed subjects on a dime, but Gilroy didn't miss a beat.

"You're stubborn, Rachel. And smart. And your kind heart gets you into trouble. But you *do* have a kind heart, and that's worth just about any price. I don't like it, but I understand why you want to help them."

It had been a long time since anyone had said anything of the sort to me. My ex-fiancé, Brent, had never been generous with his words. Telling others what he knew they needed or wanted to hear made him feel vulnerable, and he couldn't stand that. Gilroy was made of stronger stuff. I was falling in love with the man.

# CHAPTER 15

"I'm so worried about Nora," Julia said. "She could be in danger, and we're talking about ordering pizza."

"It's still daylight," I said, scrolling down a long list of search results on my computer monitor. Who knew there was so much information on Ceran St. Vrain? "We could check on her tonight. Want to?"

"I'd feel better if we did."

Holly wandered behind my desk and peered over my shoulder at the monitor. "What is it about St. Vrain you're looking for?"

"I don't know, really. I'm hoping something will jump out at me." I clicked on the Images link and the page filled with paintings, drawings, and photographs of St. Vrain, all of them of a much older man than the man in Nora's miniature. Connecting my cell phone to my computer, I downloaded the photo I'd taken of the miniature in Anne's bedroom and enlarged it on the monitor.

"Is that it?" Holly asked.

"Yes. It's on Anne Rightler's quilt. Look at that."

"What?" Holly said.

Julia joined Holly behind my chair and bent low for a better look at the monitor. "It must be said he's not a very attractive man."

I switched back to the search images. "Most of the images on the computer aren't contemporary. They're modern-day copies of a well-known painting and photograph, and they're *all* of an older St. Vrain. Really older."

"He didn't age well," Julia said.

"That must be part of Kendra's excitement over the miniature," I said. "It's not just a discovery, it's a discovery from an unchartered era in St. Vrain's life. She said the miniature was painted in 1840. That has to be twenty years earlier than this well-known painting and at least twenty-five years earlier than the photograph."

Julia straightened and wandered over to my office's only window. "It's getting darker," she announced.

"If this miniature is so much earlier, how do they know it's of St. Vrain?" Holly asked.

"Good question." I went back to my photo of the miniature. "It looks like him, though. He has a very distinctive mouth." I leaned back in my chair, studying the miniature, my thoughts taking off in a new direction. "I'd say it's St. Vrain. But then so are all these other images I've been looking at."

"Someone's parking in front of your house," Julia said, a hint of alarm in her voice. "A woman's getting out. I think it's Sheila Larson."

"You two stay up here," I said.

"What if she's the one who broke into your house?" Holly said. "She could be dangerous."

"Holly, can you really picture her using a crowbar to pry the molding from my back door? Stay here, please. I want her to talk to me."

I jogged downstairs and made it to the front door just

as Sheila rang the doorbell. Not wanting to appear overeager, I paused before opening the door. "Sheila, come in. How can I help you?"

"That's what I've come for. Your help."

I offered to take her coat, but she declined. "Can I get you coffee or tea?"

"No, I have to say this right away or I won't be able to say it at all."

I gritted my teeth, anticipating an argument or a chewing out.

She walked restlessly about my living room, finally taking a seat at my repeated encouragement. "All right, I'll just say it."

I sat down on the opposite couch. "Whatever you need to say, Sheila. I won't criticize."

She nodded, and with trembling fingers, she undid the buttons on her coat. "I'm sorry I was rude to you and Julia," she began. "I just couldn't believe . . . I wanted to believe you were lying, but I knew you weren't."

"About the drawing I found in Nora's couch?"

"Yes. The truth is, Dominic *did* ask me to change seats at Nora's, and I knew deep down he was up to something. I've tried to ignore it, but he's done it before. I've found things in our house that I know don't belong to him."

"Like what?"

"An old Indian drawing on notebook paper and an old letter by some relative of this St. Vrain person. And yesterday I found jewelry."

"A gold locket?"

"Yes! How did you know?"

"Did you by any chance take it to Aspen Glen?"

"I hid it in Anne's room on Friday. I thought if I could

make it look like Anne took it, no one would suspect Dominic, and then I could make him stop." Her voice was choked with shame and regret. "I was going to blame a dead woman."

"Why do you think Dominic takes these things?"

"He's afraid of the future. People aren't investing like they used to, so they don't need him. He's always talked about Nora having much more money than we'll ever have. He was so angry at Thanksgiving, after he found out Nora let Kendra insure the miniature. He thought it was a slap in the face. And in a way, he was right."

"But Nora had to do what she thought was right."

"It's not Nora, it's Kendra and Ben. I know it. They talked her into going with Williams and Associates, the big art insurer. Did it really matter who insured it? No. But those two got a lot of pleasure out of taking away Dominic's referral fee."

"Would they be so petty?"

Sheila looked at me with wonderment. How could I have failed to notice the most prominent aspect of their personalities? "Without a doubt. Especially Ben. He fancies himself a great historian and art connoisseur."

"So the arguments between Dominic and Ben go a long way back?"

"Ever since they met at Nora's house."

"At Thanksgiving, did you all see Anne take the miniature?"

"Nora and I did. Dominic and the Wallaces were too busy arguing."

"But you told Dominic she took it?"

Sheila nodded. "He used to get angry when Anne took things, but he laughed when he found out about the miniature. He said it served all of them right and he hoped she broke it and they couldn't collect on the insurance because Nora never took any measures to stop Anne from stealing. He said if something happened to the miniature, he'd call Williams and Associates himself and tell them Nora didn't protect it. And then when it disappeared, he was ready to call, the day after Thanksgiving."

"Did he?"

"No."

"That would only hurt Nora."

"And by then, it had been found."

Despite Dominic's genial veneer when I first met him at Thanksgiving, when he argued with Ben, he struck me as a resentful man. A man who could hold a grudge for years. Though not necessarily act on it. I had to ask. "Do you think Dominic had anything to do with Anne's or Paige's death?"

Sheila exhaled as though I'd knocked the air out of her. "What a question."

"Would he have pushed Anne down the stairs?"

She got up and walked to the far side of the room, fleeing the conversation. But the expression on her face told me she had once considered the possibility. She had *needed* to consider it in order to be free of it. She wheeled back. "No, he's not capable. He's never been violent. I would have known if he'd pushed that poor old woman down the stairs. He couldn't have kept it from me."

"And Paige?"

A faint smile crossed her lips. "I think he was working with Paige. He wouldn't want to kill her."

I'd long suspected that Paige wasn't alone in stealing the miniature. I couldn't imagine her wrestling Anne for it. "So Dominic *did* take the miniature?"

"No, he didn't," she said, vigorously shaking her head. "Paige must have. Dominic saw Anne take it, but when it wasn't found on her body, he was as shocked as I was. Looking back, he probably thought Paige was working without him. But I bet Paige took the other things I found in our house."

"Then how did Paige end up with the miniature?" I was thinking aloud, not expecting an answer. Because *that* was the question. Whoever took the miniature from Anne had killed her for it.

"I can only tell you what I believe," Sheila said, "and that's that Dominic isn't a killer and he didn't steal the miniature." She plopped down on the couch, exhausted from her confessions.

"You said you wanted my help?"

"Could you talk to Dominic and Chief Gilroy?"

"Sheila, I don't think—"

"Act as a go-between so he can return the letter without being arrested?"

"Gilroy isn't going to want to hear from *me* about this. Dominic will to have to face the chief himself. And what about the drawing he took?"

Sheila's countenance changed in that moment. I'd dashed her hopes. "He's selling it today. I don't know how to stop him. We have an early dinner meeting with a buyer, supposedly for an old family painting, but that painting isn't worth more than two hundred dollars. I saw an envelope taped to the back of the painting."

"The drawing was in it."

"Clever, isn't it?" She began to button her coat. "I'm sorry I bothered you," she said, barely able to raise her chin. "I just don't know what to do."

I felt sorry for her, and my sympathy was going to get me into trouble, I just knew it. "When and where are you having dinner?"

She glanced up at me. "Wyatt's at five o'clock. Dominic doesn't want to spend money on a fancy restaurant."

"I might be able to say something to him."

"Oh, thank you!"

"Sheila, I don't have much of a plan. Get there early, before the buyer. I'll tell Dominic what I know, but not how I know it. Hopefully it will scare him into returning the drawing before the buyer shows up. But don't bet on it."

"I think it will work."

I had to be honest with her. I'd called it a plan, but it was nothing half as lofty as that. "I don't. I think he'll get angry and tell me to shove off. But that's where you come in, Sheila. You're his wife. I can only start the ball rolling, and I'm not sure I should even do that."

"Please," she said, getting up from the couch. "It may sound funny, but I think he'll listen to you. You know about things, and I . . . don't."

"Don't say that."

"Just *please*. I'll get us there about fifteen minutes early. I'll make up an excuse. Maybe ten minutes, but no later than that."

"One question. Do you or Dominic know what will happen to Nora's collection when she dies?"

"Everyone knows. Nora's made it clear. It's to be sold, and the proceeds will go to the Aspen Glen assisted living home. That's why Kendra is so crazed about cataloging it as fast as possible. She's trying to talk Nora into donating records and artifacts to the museum, or selling them to finance the museum, one piece at a time. I think she's succeeded in some cases."

"You say everyone knows. Dominic, Kendra, and Ben?"

"She told us all."

"Thanks. I'll see you at Wyatt's."

No doubt thinking I was about to change my mind about meeting her at Wyatt's, she scurried out the door.

My thoughts in a whirl, I stood in the living room, wondering what had possessed me to agree to meet Dominic. Yet one good thing would come of Dominic's meeting with the buyer, I thought. He wouldn't be knocking on Nora's door tonight. He'd be too busy to do that—and too happy with his payoff. But that still left Kendra and Ben as threats to her safety.

I heard footsteps clomping on the wooden floors of my office. "You are *not* going alone," Holly shouted down the stairs.

# CHAPTER 16

True to her word, Sheila was seated with Dominic at a corner table in Wyatt's when I got there, fifteen minutes before five. I'd left Holly and Julia in the car, joking that they were to come and get me if I didn't come out in fifteen minutes. Julia had not been amused.

As I started for the table, a large, barrel-chested man strode through the door behind me, passed me by, and walked with swift intent toward the Larsons.

"Sheila and Dominic, how are you?" he bellowed, turning heads at nearby tables.

I froze twenty feet from the table. Sheila saw me. With a look of desperation in her eyes, she shouted, "How good to see you, Rachel!" Before Dominic could say a word, she was at my side, hauling me toward the table.

"I'm sorry to interrupt," I said.

Sheila pushed down on my shoulders, forcing me to sit. "Nonsense. Mr. Travers, meet my friend Rachel Stowe."

"How do you do?" he said, looking from me to Dominic.

"This is a private dinner," Dominic said.

Sheila balked. "Don't be rude. I won't have you be rude anymore."

"Am *I* interrupting something?" Travers said. "I can

wait."

"You're not interrupting anything," Dominic replied. "Let's settle business."

I decided to leap in. "Mr. Travers, what do you do for a living?"

With a bemused smile on his face, as if to say, *Okay, I'll play this game*, he said, "I insure art."

"With a company?"

"A company, of course. I doubt you've heard of them. Williams and Associates."

You could have knocked me over with a feather. And I wasn't alone. Sheila was gaping at Travers. I kicked her under the table and recovered myself as best I could. "I understand your company recently insured Nora Barberton's miniature of Ceran St. Vrain."

Travers pulled in his chin, staring at me as though he couldn't believe I possessed such information. "They did, for quite a sum. How do you know about that?"

"Rachel and I are friends," Sheila said.

"It's the first time I've heard of it," Dominic said. He was glaring at me with the same intensity he'd stared at Ben during Thanksgiving. Was he as dangerous as he looked? Or were his black looks all bluster?

"You don't know all my friends," Sheila said, brushing his arm with her fingers. "I have my own life, Dominic."

Dominic chuckled and looked at Sheila. "I do know all your friends, like you know mine. I also know the people you can't stand, and Rachel's one of them."

"That's so rude!"

"It's so true."

"I never said that. Rachel, I never said that."

Travers was shifting his attention from one Larson to

the other and back again, as if he were at an all-Larson tennis match. The smile had vanished from his lips.

"Mr. Travers, do you insure anything else of Nora's?" I asked.

He paused, thrown off balance a tad by the quick change of topic. "I wish I did, Rachel. She's a wonderful woman with a breathtaking collection."

I nodded my agreement. "She *is* nice, and I've seen her collection. Diaries, letters, the miniature . . . ledger books."

Travers stared.

Oblivious to the new subject at the table, Dominic said, "Mr. Travers, would you like to meet elsewhere? Anywhere."

"We're staying here," Sheila said.

"That's enough," Dominic snarled. "I told you I have business to conduct. What are you doing?"

"I agree," Travers said. "That's enough." He pushed out from the table, his chair making a scraping sound on the floor.

"Mr. Travers, I'm ready to do business," Dominic pleaded.

"I believe you are," Travers said. "But is your wife? And now that I think of it, am I?"

"This is between you and me," Dominic said.

"I don't think so," Travers said. "It seems there's a third party I wasn't aware of. Had I been aware, I never would have agreed to our meeting." He pushed from the table another few inches and stood. "Ladies, nice to meet you. Dominic, perhaps someday. Something with a *different* provenance."

Travers made his way out of the restaurant as swiftly as he'd entered, and I pursued him to the sidewalk, calling his name.

"I didn't mean to ruin your dinner," I said. In my peripheral vision I saw Holly and Julia hovering around the hood of my Forester, Holly yanking on Julia's arm to keep her by the car.

"Not at all," Travers said. "Thank you for saving me from a business deal I'd regret—should I have ever discovered the true nature of the deal."

"Can I ask you something?" I said.

"Go right ahead. I owe you one."

"Have you seen Nora's miniature?"

"I have."

"What do you think?"

"About what?"

"About its provenance."

He smiled. "It's perhaps a little shaky."

"But you insured it."

"My company did, on the advice of Kendra Wallace, who had her own reasons, I'm sure, for authenticating it. Like that museum of hers. But we accepted her advice." He shrugged a shoulder. "She's the expert, and I'm only the insurer."

"Do you think Dominic knows how shaky its provenance is?"

"Between you and me, he hasn't got a clue. Neither does dear Nora."

"So Dominic doesn't—"

"Dominic had nothing to do with the provenance of that miniature, you can be sure of that."

"Do you know who did?"

"No, and I wouldn't want to. They did a shoddy job."

"But Nora—"

"Doesn't need to know anything. I've heard Kendra Wallace wants to buy it for her historical society—or she wants Nora to donate it, in which case it's a tax write-off. Nora will need all the money she can in the near future, and either way, I want her to have it."

"Do you know about her, well, problems?"

"Yes, ma'am, I know. Nice to meet you, Rachel Stowe."

Travers tipped his head, walked a few steps, and then pivoted back. "Dominic isn't a *bad* man, Rachel. But then, I don't think I am, either."

"Neither do I, Mr. Travers."

"Say hello to Nora for me." Travers grinned and headed down the sidewalk, and I walked over to Holly and Julia, who had at last settled down, realizing I wasn't going to be strangled in the restaurant. "Well?" Holly said.

"I'll tell you in the car." I twisted back for a peek through Wyatt's window. Dominic and Sheila were still at their table, Dominic massaging his temples, looking more crushed than angry, and Sheila trying to console him. Maybe he wasn't a bad man. Maybe just a desperate and reckless one.

I got into my car, started the engine to get the heat going, and told Holly and Julia about the brief but strange meeting with Travers.

"I don't know how I feel about this," Holly said. "Travers deals in stolen art."

"But not Nora's art," I said.

"He's still a thief," Julia declared. "You're going to let him off the hook?"

"There's no hook, Julia," I said. "I'm not the police, and he didn't take the ledger drawing from Dominic. He did nothing illegal in Wyatt's. Anyway, I have a feeling that drawing will end up back at Nora's very soon."

"I hope you're right. She's being taken advantage of."

"Not by Travers, she isn't. Should we stop for pizza?"

"If we take Nora some," Julia said. "We were going to look in on her."

We phoned Nora and ordered two pizzas from Bella Vita's on Orchard Street. Fifteen minutes later we were on our way to her house. She was happy to see us and had set the table with plates, napkins, and a bottle of wine. I told the others to get started and asked Nora if I could snoop around her documents room for a few minutes. A few steps up the stairs, I paused. "Nora, a Mr. Travers says to say hello."

"He's in town? How lovely! How did you meet him?"

"I ran into him at Wyatt's. I understand he works for Williams and Associates."

"That's one of the reasons I went with them to insure the miniature. What a nice man. And he's quite an art expert, even though he works in insurance. I had him here earlier this month for dinner, and we had such a lovely time." She leaned close. "I was having a bad day. While we were in the kitchen, I forgot for a moment which cabinet my coffee was in, and later I couldn't remember where I put my water glass and napkin. It only lasted a very short time, but I was upset and blurted out what was wrong. He treated me with such grace."

Upstairs in the documents room, I looked to the cabinet shelf where the miniature had once sat, remembering how excited Kendra had been to present it to Nora's guests. Travers must have known the moment he laid eyes on it that it was a fake, but he'd accepted Kendra's assessment of its authenticity, which he also knew to be fake, for Nora's sake.

So she could sell the miniature and put away the money for her future. He'd risked his job, his reputation, for her. I didn't like his side business—buying stolen artifacts—but I wasn't going to waste more time wondering if I'd done the right thing by not telling Gilroy about him.

Kendra had also been willing to risk her reputation, but for a much less honorable end. She wanted that miniature for her museum. Ben wanted it for his dissertation, the "hard, original evidence" Dominic had told me he needed. That dissertation would give Ben the recognition and admiration he felt was his due. But were the Wallaces thieves like Dominic? Were they killers?

I opened Kendra's catalog file on the computer, the one she'd opened earlier in the day while Nora and I watched, and soon discovered that it was easy to manipulate. With a few keystrokes I deleted an item, and with another few, I restored it. No password was required, no administrative authority. As many times as Dominic had been in the documents room, and no doubt watched Kendra catalog her findings, he must have known how to remove items he wanted to steal from Kendra's list.

"Pizza?"

I turned to see Holly in the doorway, plate in hand. "Thanks, I'm famished," I said.

"I like Nora. Does she live alone in this big house?" Holly entered the room, glanced over the cluttered shelves, and then found a bare spot on the desk for the plate.

"She *lives* alone, but she's not alone, if you know what I mean. A lot of people care about her."

"What a royal mess. What are you looking for?"

"The answers to two important questions. First, were Kendra and Ben also stealing from Nora? And second, who killed Anne and Paige?"

"You think you'll find the answers in here?"

I stared at the wedge of pizza in my hand. "I think I just figured out that Kendra isn't the thief." It was obvious, now that I thought about it. Why would Kendra enter an artifact into her database and delete it later, taking a chance that someone might see it in the database in the meantime and wonder where it had gone? No, if Kendra wanted to steal, she'd steal. She wouldn't take the extra, dangerous step of removing items from her files. She'd put the drawing or the letter in her purse and stroll out the door, never entering it into her database. And Ben would do the same as Kendra. Only Dominic, who didn't create the files, would have to alter them.

"That's progress. But Dominic's a thief for sure," Holly said. "Do you think he was the only one of the four?"

I considered the question, rolled it over in my mind, stacked it up against what I had learned since meeting the Wallaces and Larsons. "Yes, Dominic was the only one. I'm positive. Kendra had nothing to gain by stealing from Nora. Her whole focus is that museum, and she can't display stolen items in it, she can only persuade Nora to donate or sell pieces of her collection."

"What about Ben?"

"I don't think he cares very much about the collection, except as a research tool. He doesn't feel the need to own any of it."

"If Dominic is the thief, could he be the one who broke into your house?"

"No." I shook my head, certain of my conclusion.

"Good. Then when you get your door fixed, you can sleep easy."

I felt a tightness in my stomach. I knew I wasn't going to sleep easy, or at all. "I wish you were right, Holly. But the person who broke into my house also killed Anne and Paige."

# CHAPTER 17

We split up, Julia staying with Nora, and Holly and me climbing into my Forester and speeding off for Dominic and Sheila's house, using the address provided by Nora. I'd become convinced that Dominic and that miniature held the key to who had killed Anne and Paige. It was a shot in the dark, but I had to take it. Nora was safe. In fact, for Kendra and Ben, she was only valuable alive. If she died before Kendra had finished cataloging her collection and begging for artifacts, Kendra and her museum would get nothing. And Ben's gold mine of records for his dissertation would vanish.

But I wasn't safe. The killer had broken into my home, my peaceful Juniper Grove home, to warn me to back off, and I wasn't about to back off. Gilroy was right about that: I was stubborn.

The Larson home was a brick ranch on Apple Blossom Lane, five blocks south of downtown. The streetlights were on, and behind the drapes in the picture window, warm lights shone. I pulled into the drive, just behind the Larsons' black sedan, leaned forward, and looked out the windshield. The curtains fluttered. I'd either be allowed inside, sulkily, or told in no uncertain terms to get off the property. "Holly, wait here, all right?"

"Are you sure?"

"I'll be fine. Dominic's going to be hard enough to talk to without—"

"Bringing a friend along for the show," Holly finished.

"Exactly."

By the time I reached the front door, Sheila had opened it and was welcoming me inside. I caught sight of Dominic glowering on an old wing-backed chair in the living room, but he made no move to stop me or his wife.

"I'm sorry to stop by without calling first," I began.

"But you wanted to catch us by surprise," Dominic said. "That seems to be your modus operandi."

Sheila motioned for me to sit next to her on a couch. "Actually, we wanted to thank you, didn't we, Dominic?"

Dominic grunted.

"We're turning over a new leaf," she said.

"A penniless leaf," Dominic added.

"It beats a prison leaf," Sheila said. There was a strength in her tone that I hadn't heard before, and curiously, Dominic wasn't debating her or making faces. "Rachel, I've been trying to convince my husband that you don't plan to turn him in to the police. Am I right?"

"You're right. I haven't said anything, and I don't intend to."

"Thank you for that," Dominic said.

"Though I think Nora would like it if you returned anything you took from the documents room."

"Already done," Dominic said. Clearly he was still smarting from his loss, but at the same time, I saw a lightness in his demeanor that was hard to put a finger on. He wasn't so . . . frantic. "I mailed a drawing and letter I took. She'll get them on Monday."

I grinned. "That's great."

"Sorry if I can't be so happy," Dominic said. He looked away. "I've got a mortgage to pay and no job."

"I wouldn't be so sure about that," I said. "Nora can be very forgiving. That's something I've learned about her."

"Forgiving of *stealing* from her?" Sheila asked.

"It's not forgiveness if it's over something inconsequential," I said. "I don't think she'll tell your bank, Dominic. You won't lose your job there."

Dominic looked back, his eyes riveted to mine. "She won't?"

"Do you hear that?" Sheila said.

"She's not a vindictive person. About working for her as a financial adviser, though, I'm not so sure. Maybe, maybe not. Would you mind if I talked to her?"

"I wouldn't mind at all. Do you think she might rehire me?"

"I'm not promising anything, but I have a feeling she will. Though it might take a week or two for her to calm down."

"That's not a problem at all," Dominic said. "Three or four weeks, in fact. And I wouldn't blame her if she never forgave me. I owe her a lot. Please tell her I'd be very grateful to work for her again, and I'll answer any questions she has about what I did. I hate that I took her things. I got . . . I was . . ."

"Afraid for our financial future," Sheila said. "We're struggling."

"I was going to stop after I took the first ledger drawing," Dominic went on, "but I was so angry on Thanksgiving when I found out she wasn't going to let me insure the St. Vrain miniature. That was money right out of my pocket." He pressed his fingers over his eyes, as if to block the memory of that night. "Of all the stupid things I've ever done. Of all the people to hurt."

"Then again," I said, "Nora isn't going to be so forgiving of the person who murdered her friend Anne, and Paige."

Sheila shot me a wounded look. "You can't think we had anything to do with killing those two."

"I don't, Sheila. But I think Dominic can help me find out who did. I just need the truth."

Dominic sat forward, ready to talk, eager to assuage his conscience. "I'll help any way I can."

"Then I need an honest answer to this question. Did you ever suspect that the miniature was a fake?"

Dominic examined his hands, rubbing his fingers, buying time to consider my question. "I have to admit I thought it was a fake the first time I saw it," he said at last.

Sheila's jaw dropped. "It's fake? That stupid little painting that everyone is after and argues about all the time?"

"Maybe a pretty good fake, I don't know," Dominic said. "I'm not a great judge of forgeries. It's real ivory, and it looks old, but it's hard to believe no one in the field of history or art knew of its existence until now." He shrugged. "I sensed something was wrong with it, but I was hoping to insure it, so I didn't say anything. I wouldn't be surprised to learn that someone took the paint off an old and worthless miniature and used it for St. Vrain's portrait."

"You sound like you know how it was done," I said.

Dominic raised his hands. "Hold on, I've never done that. Trying to sell to Travers was as far as I've gone. I don't do forgeries."

"I believe you, but I get the feeling you know who

*does*. Where would Ben go if he wanted to create an undiscovered miniature circa 1820?"

"Ben?" Sheila said, looking from me to Dominic.

"Kendra had very little to gain by forging a miniature," I explained. "It added to the prestige of Nora's collection, and to the museum if she could obtain it, but the danger in paying someone to create it wasn't worth it to her. She already had the rest of Nora's collection—or what parts of it she could talk Nora into giving away or selling. But Ben needed a kicker for his dissertation. Something undiscovered."

Dominic's mouth tightened. "A new St. Vrain time line. He went on and on about that. He'd promised it to his dissertation director."

"Would he create the forgery himself?" I asked.

"He's not capable," Dominic said. "But he knows an artist. He talked about him once, very briefly. And when I asked about him again the next day, he clammed up. I think he was sorry he mentioned him."

"Who is this artist?"

"He lives in Juniper Grove. Martin Coyle."

"You think Ben did more than create a forgery," Sheila said. "I can see it in your face."

I swallowed hard, aware I was about to accuse a man of a terrible crime. "I believe he shoved Anne down the stairs and killed Paige in her apartment, after he went there to retrieve the miniature."

"You think Ben would kill two women? I don't believe it," Dominic said, defending him for probably the first time in his life. "I can't stand the guy, but I don't see him as a murderer."

"Think about it, Dominic. It was either you, Sheila,

Ben, or Kendra who killed them. Nora didn't do it. And Paige didn't or she wouldn't be dead now. Ben killed Paige because of what she knew—or more likely, saw."

A long pause ensued, during which I imagined Dominic was about to toss me out of his house. But I could see his gears turning, see I was making sense to him, though he didn't want to admit the truth of what I was saying. Ben was worse than an arrogant dolt who loved to tweak his and Sheila's noses. He was a cold-hearted killer. "Tell me something, then. Why did Paige have the miniature? Doesn't that prove she stole it?"

"If she was the one who stole it from Anne," I said, "why didn't she keep it? Instead, she returned it—at her own risk. I think she saw Ben hide it before the police arrived. When Paige took things, she took them from the *house*, not Nora's guests."

"I guess." Dominic winced a little. He knew what I was getting ready to ask him.

"This is extremely important, Dominic. Did you work with Paige to steal things from Nora's house?"

He looked at Sheila, and she gave him an encouraging tip of the head. "Go ahead. Tell her. I know more than you think I know."

"Okay." Dominic was resigned to spilling it all, I could tell. He wanted to be free of the burden he had placed on his own shoulders. "Yes, we worked together. Paige heard noises in Nora's bedroom a couple weeks ago. During one of Nora's dinner parties. I'd gone up there, saying I was going into the documents room, but I took a gold locket from Nora's dresser. When I turned around to leave, Paige was at the door. In exchange for her keeping quiet, I agreed to cut her in on whatever I could sell. But I'm telling you, I've returned everything. I don't know what happened to the locket."

"I found it and took it to Anne's old room at Aspen Glen," Sheila said.

Dominic drew in his breath. "I thought it disappeared. I looked and couldn't find it anywhere."

"I knew Chief Gilroy or someone at the home would find it there and give it to Nora."

Now I was more convinced than ever that Ben had killed both women. Dominic had had ample opportunity to kill Paige but had never acted. If he was a killer, I thought, he would have strangled her when she first threatened to reveal what he was doing. Instead, he had agreed to give her part of his money. Travers was right. Dominic wasn't a truly bad man. Just a hurting man who had made bad decisions.

"Wait," Sheila said. "If Paige saw Ben hide the miniature, then she knew he killed Anne. The only way Ben could've taken it from her was to kill her."

"I'm afraid you're right," I said. "It's possible Paige thought she could sell it on her own and not cut Dominic in. I think she was filled with remorse later, thinking about Anne, and that's why she took it to Aspen Glen. But by then Ben had figured out that only Paige could have taken the miniature out of the house. When I told Kendra and Ben that Paige had used mashed potatoes to do it, Kendra was worried about damage to the miniature. Ben wasn't. He tried to calm her down. Dissertation or no dissertation, he wasn't upset. I think he realized at that moment that he was better off with a *stolen* forgery. But he couldn't trust Paige to let it remain stolen. He knew it would pop up again—at an auction, in a private sale."

"I see," Dominic said. "He had photos of it for his new

time line, and Kendra's verification, but no actual miniature to come back and bite him. He could claim for the rest of his life that he'd discovered something new about St. Vrain, and no one could ever counter him."

I got to my feet. "Dominic, you need to come with me to the police station. Gilroy needs to know about you, Paige, and Ben. This needs to end right now. Ben broke into my house today. He's a dangerous man."

"Are you all right?" Sheila asked.

"I wasn't there, thank goodness, and he only broke my back door, but he won't stop at a break-in. He's after me. Dominic?"

"You want me to tell the police I've stolen from Nora," Dominic began, rising from his chair, staring ever downward at me as he stood taller and taller. "They'll arrest me."

"Not if Nora doesn't press charges," I said. "Gilroy's focus will be on Ben, not you."

"I'll go with you," Sheila told Dominic. "We owe Nora and Rachel."

"I can't risk it. I'll lose my job at the bank. I'll lose all my clients."

"You have to trust Nora not to press charges," I said. "Do the right thing and return her trust in the only way you can right now."

Sheila touched his arm. "And return my trust, Dominic."

Dominic grabbed his and Sheila's coat, helped her on with hers, and raced out the front door. *Those long legs could outrun a greyhound*, I thought.

# CHAPTER 18

After church, I took two dozen of Holly's heavenly donuts to Aspen Glen. Donna, Betty, and Frank—especially Betty—had remembered my promise to bring them and swarmed about the coffee table, choosing chocolate, glazed, and blueberry jelly from the pink box. Before church I'd eaten the cream puff Holly had brought me yesterday, so I was able to resist temptation. Well, I was able to resist a *second* temptation.

Donna took her prize to her seat closest to the fire, Betty sat beside her, and I sat on the facing couch, next to Frank. "Did you hear Anne's killer confessed?" I asked them.

"No one told us," Betty said. "Who was it?"

"It happened last night, so it's not in the paper," I said. "It was Ben Wallace, a lecturer at Northern Colorado Community College."

"Why would he want to kill Anne?" Donna asked. "She never hurt anyone."

"Never hurt a soul," Frank said.

"It's so unfair," Betty added.

Their confusion, a byproduct of their innocence and kindness, made my heart heavy. I explained as best I could why Ben had taken Anne's life, but again I didn't mention

Paige. They hadn't heard that she, too, was killed, and there was no point in telling them. Anne's murder was enough sadness for them to bear.

"Did that handsome police chief arrest him?"

I turned. Behind me was the wisp of a woman I'd seen two days ago—the interloper who had placed herself between Betty and Gilroy on the couch.

"Yes, he did," I told her. "And locked him up."

She edged closer to the back of the couch. "Are those donuts for everyone?"

"Absolutely."

Frank lifted the box and balanced it on the back of the couch, holding it there until the woman made her choice.

"Tell him for us that we're grateful he caught that man," Betty said. "I feel safer knowing he's the chief."

"Me too," I said. "He's a good man."

Gilroy had sent me a text message late last night, as Holly, Julia, and I sat in Nora's house, unable to sleep, our imaginations working overtime with what might be happening to Dominic and Ben: "Paid Mr. Wallace a visit. He was with forger. Confessed. Mrs. Wallace angry, didn't know about forgery. Get feeling she thought it might be fake and didn't care. Suppose that's not a criminal offense."

That text message was as much as he'd ever told me about a case before it made it to the courts. I smiled when I saw it, and smiled again remembering it. And then Gilroy had texted that he'd asked friends of his to repair my door on Monday at a big discount. He hoped he wasn't sticking his nose in. Was it all right with me? I had texted back that it was more than all right.

A few minutes later, remembering Dominic and his predicament, I'd texted Gilroy again: "Please don't arrest

Dominic. Nora doesn't want you to. She knows everything he did."

Julia had rolled her eyes through the entire exchange. "There are such things as phones," she'd said.

Nora had told me she would call the station first thing in the morning, to make sure there were no charges against Dominic. And she would take Dominic back in a few days, but only as her financial adviser. He wasn't to set foot in the documents room or any place other than her kitchen. For now, her collection was off-limits to everyone. Maybe one day a college student writing a paper would be allowed to search the documents. Maybe.

"It's snowing," Betty said, pointing at the windows overlooking the parking lot.

I twisted back in my seat. Fat flakes drifted lazily to the ground, and a thin layer of snow shimmered on the asphalt. I thought of the Kiss in the Snow and grinned. Broadly enough that Frank asked me what I was laughing about.

"I'm just happy, Frank. Mind if I have a donut?"

"You go right ahead," Donna said. "You have as many as you want. What kind do you like?"

"Jelly. Like you," I said, reaching into the box. Boy, was I overdoing it on the sweets. But I wanted to celebrate, and celebrate I would.

"It's going to be Christmas before we know it," Frank said, shaking his head in dismay. "I have to go shopping for all my grandchildren."

"Shop online," Betty said. "That's what I do."

"I don't shop for anyone," Donna said.

Betty put an arm around her friend. "We'll shop for each other, won't we? We'll all have each other for Christmas."

I took a bite of my donut, a small one so it wouldn't ooze jelly down my coat. I even plugged the tiny hole at the back of the donut with my finger so no jelly would escape from there. I was getting better at this.

Frank jabbed my arm to get my attention and pointed toward the receptionist desk. "Martina is trying to get your attention."

Taking my donut with me, I crossed the lobby to meet with the assisted living home's director—an older woman herself, maybe no more than twenty years from an assisted living home. *Good*, I thought. *Better than a younger person. She knows what the residents go through.*

"Martina Oliver," she said, giving me her hand. "I'm the director of Aspen Glen. I've been hearing about your donuts, Rachel."

"Hi," I said, shaking her hand with my free one. "They're Holly Kavanagh's. From Holly's Sweets."

Martina's hand went to her collarbone. "Oh, straight from the gates of heaven. I can't resist."

I glanced sheepishly down at my hand. "Neither can I."

"I've also heard how you helped Nora Barberton, and I wanted to thank you."

"I didn't really help her."

"That's not what I heard. She called me first thing this morning and told me you'd solved Anne Rightler's murder." She laughed when she saw my questioning look. "Not that Nora keeps me informed on everything, but we chat almost every morning. We're old friends."

"Poor Anne. All she wanted to do was protect something precious that belonged to her friend, and she died for it. It's a shame Nora's historical collection was in such bad hands, at least for a time."

"Those so-called friends of hers," Martina said gruffly. "They didn't give a fig about her. All they cared about was her money."

"Her money and that ugly miniature."

Martina's lips curved into a smile. "Nora told me about the miniature. As soon as the insurance company appraised it, she decided to sell it and give the proceeds to Aspen Glen. She told me not to tell her cataloger if I ever met her."

I wondered if Martina knew the miniature was a fake. And I quickly decided it wasn't my place to tell her. "Nora needs to save some of that money for herself, I think," I said as delicately as possible. "For her future, I mean."

"I know that," Martina replied, touching my forearm, letting me know without saying so that she knew Nora's secret. "Nora has a place at Aspen Glen, whenever she needs it and for as long as she needs it. Free of charge, approved by the board."

"Really? That's wonderful."

"The board decided yesterday, and I told Nora when we talked this morning. But with all she's done for us?" Martina nodded. "You bet she's welcome here. In a way, she's paid for her stay many times over. And she's still helping us. She asked Donna to dinner this Friday." Martina lowered her voice. "You've met Donna. She doesn't have any family. No one visits her."

"Now she has family," I said, my eyes traveling back to the fireplace, where Donna, Betty, and Frank ate their donuts, talked, and laughed. "And she has friends."

Martina excused herself and I stood for a moment by the receptionist desk, watching the snow fall. I had much to be thankful for. Not turkey and mashed potatoes, but good friends and James Gilroy.

"Are you going to eat that?" the receptionist asked me, staring with covetous desire at my donut.

"Oh, yeah. But there are more in a box near the fireplace, so help yourself." I took a large bite, and a glob of blueberry jelly hit my coat. "No, no. What is wrong with me? I don't believe it! Do you have a paper towel or napkin?"

The receptionist searched her desk top. "Sorry, no. Nothing."

I swept up the glob with my fingers, did the only thing I could do with it—eat it—and dashed out to my car for some paper towels I kept in the cargo area. This coat was too new, too precious. Why had I chosen blueberry? Nothing ruined fabric better.

Ten feet from my Forester, I ran into Gilroy and froze like a statue. There I was, my fingers stained blue, my coat with a big blue stain on it. I was reliving the embarrassing and all-too-recent past.

"Blueberry again?" he said, his eyes twinkling.

"You must think I have an obsession."

"I think you know your mind when it comes to donuts, and there's nothing wrong with that."

I gestured at the car door. "I need a paper towel."

"You forget I have a handkerchief," he said, pulling one from his suit jacket and putting it in my hand.

I wiped my fingers and then my coat, making a rather hopeless face as I did the latter.

"I know a cleaner who can get blueberry out," he said.

"You know a lot of people." I gave up on the paper towel and let my hands drop. "Thank you for calling someone to fix my door."

"No problem."

The snow swirled around my car, driven by a gust of

wind, and then settled again, falling gently to the ground.

"I think it's long past time we had our Thanksgiving dinner."

"I agree."

And then he put his arm around me, lowered his face to mine, and kissed me in the snow.

## FROM THE AUTHOR

We all need a place to escape to from time to time. A place where neighbors drink cups of coffee around a kitchen table (and some indulge in cream puffs), where friends feel safe sharing their hearts' deepest yearnings, where neighbors stop to chat with neighbors outside flower shops. True, the occasional murder mars the Juniper Grove landscape, but what would a mystery series be without dead bodies? Juniper Grove is still that place of escape, and I hope you'll join me there for all the books in the series. I look forward to sharing more of Rachel Stowe and her friends with you.

If you enjoyed *At Death's Door*, please consider leaving a review on Amazon. Nothing fancy, just a couple sentences. Your help is appreciated more than I can say. Reviews make a huge difference in helping readers find the Juniper Grove Mystery Series and in allowing me to continue to write the series. Thank you!

## KARIN'S MAILING LIST

For giveaways, exclusive content, and the latest news on the Juniper Grove Mystery Series and future Karin Kaufman books, sign up to the mail and newsletter list at KarinKaufman.com.

## MORE BOOKS BY KARIN KAUFMAN

ANNA DENNING MYSTERY SERIES

The Witch Tree
Sparrow House
The Sacrifice
The Club
Bitter Roots
Anna Denning Mystery Series Box Set: Books 1-3

CHILDREN'S BOOKS (FOR CHILDREN AND ADULTS)

The Adventures of Geraldine Woolkins

## OTHER BOOKS IN THE JUNIPER GROVE MYSTERY SERIES

Death of a Dead Man
Death of a Scavenger
At Death's Door
Death of a Santa
Scared to Death
Cheating Death
Death Trap
Death Knell

Made in the USA
Columbia, SC
30 October 2021